The Other Shore

T0286109

The Other Shore

Hoa Pham

Goldsmiths
Press

Printed and bound by Short Run Press Limited, UK
Distribution by the MIT Press
Cambridge, Massachusetts, USA and London, England

ISBN 978-1-913380-82-3 (pbk)
ISBN 978-1-913380-81-6 (ebk)

www.gold.ac.uk/goldsmiths-press

Goldsmiths
UNIVERSITY OF LONDON

"scattered to the winds
Are the seeds of my good heart
Each branching connected to the source
To see with the eyes of compassion"
– an ancestral lineage poem

My name is Kim Nguyen. I'm sixteen years old and my secret middle name is from a poem that means "of good heart" in Vietnamese. I have kept many things I see and hear to myself. This protects me, being a plain, ordinary schoolgirl in uniform, a white áo dài that is impossible to keep clean. I do not show off at school, because the pressure of the student competition and the ritual picking on the weakest students by the teachers is too much for me. I learnt about competition on the first day of high school from my best friend, Ngoc, who told me not to get angry at the teachers' jibes about me being the ugly sister.

"They will be silent after they receive a gift," she told me.

This was my first encounter with corruption – a corruption everyone expected.

In our house many people died, but all of Việt Nam bleeds ghosts from the wars. When I was growing up, I would see other white ghosts, like Americans, and would practise my English with them. Sometimes they would be wary, other times not. I have gradually learnt not to be afraid of strangers.

My family lived south of Hoan Kiem lake. When I closed my eyes at night, I heard the steady whirr of traffic going by. Hanoi only sleeps from midnight to four am. In the early morning old women like my grandmother would do tai chi on the shore of the green lake. At four am goods would be brought to the markets and to the noodle hawkers on the street. Then the traffic would ramp up and tourist touts and beggars would take to the lake, while the more affluent would lunch and eat ice cream.

In the middle of the lake is the One Temple Pagoda, fierce, with a tiger guarding it, a constant reminder of King Le Loi and the legend of the turtle that carried his sword away.

To most people I am no one. To Bà, my grandmother, I was someone special who kept her secrets.

My first memory was when I was four years old. I woke up to the sound of furious voices barely contained. Curious, I slipped off the wooden platform that I slept on with my sister and crept downstairs. I heard the slap-slap syllables of Bà when she was angry and the hiss of my father suppressed by violence.

"If you do this, we will abandon our ancestors! We will be cursed!" Bà protested.

"Come now, mother, you heard the Party edict. We can't have the shrine in our house! They'll cast us out as superstitious, send us to a re-education camp! Is that what you want for our girls? To have their parents breaking rocks in hard labour?"

Bà sighed and I knew father had won.

"We will be cursed," she said, softly crying, and I ran upstairs before the adults could spot me.

The next morning the family altar that had dominated the sitting room was gone.

The next night I woke from deep sleep at the sound of a bell. The chime was far away and for a moment I thought I was dreaming. Then I smelt incense.

Quietly I crept downstairs, where the scent was stronger. I heard the murmuring of mantras and with a leap of my heart I realised Bà had disobeyed father.

There was a pool of light under the stairs and that's where I found her, with pictures of her grandparents, my ancestors and a deceased aunt that I had never met. The scent of a single carnation offset the incense and Bà was bent over tending to the mini altar that could be hidden with a draw of a curtain.

Bà turned around and smiled, putting her finger to her lips.

"Child, bow to your ancestors."

Eager to please, I accepted the single stick of incense and bowed three times to the altar.

"The spirits are more important than the whims of men," she whispered to me.

From that day on I learnt my father was not always right and the spirits would always be with us. That night I thought I dreamt of my deceased aunt in a blue áo dài walking past the river, to cross to the other shore. It was not till I was older that I realised the full import of what I saw.

Then when I saw in another dream a stroke that killed Bà, I did not tell her because I did not want it to come true.

Saying things and naming things sometimes make things happen.

Once, I was ignorant of all this. Once, I just pinched mandarins and dragon fruit from our family ancestral altar to eat. But now I present offerings every day, knowing that someone is waiting for me on the other shore.

I did not realise how much Hanoi buoyed my spirits up, nor how free and innocent I was, until it was all taken away...

1

I was on the annual pilgrimage to the Perfume Pagoda with my high school friends. It was a girls' day out, six of us piled into a tiny rowboat with bouquets of red roses and fruit for offerings. The old woman with her bark-brown, hard skin paddled us up the river.

We paid dong to the security men lined up at the river checkpoints and gave them soft drinks and cigarette packets.

There were boys, flashy boys with their boom box, their boat lined up next to ours. One of my more flirtatious, beautiful friends chatted coyly with the most charming of them, egging him on. He stood up to our giggling and tried to climb into our boat.

He slipped and fell. Clutching desperately, flailing, he reached out and pulled me into the water.

I could not swim. Weighed down by my clunky high heels and tight jeans I scrabbled desperately in the murky, green water. My feet found no footing and I tangled up in weeds and a net. Sound became distant. I could see my best friend leaning over the water.

No one would notice if I was gone…

I was only the second daughter, sixteen, plain, single, and had never had a boyfriend. No one really cared about me but my grandmother Bà, and she was dead, gone to the other shore two years ago…

…I was cradled by softness and white light…

I am Kim Nguyen. There are generations of us going back centuries, when Việt Nam had only six names. My middle name was chosen from a line in a poem that indicates what generation I am from.

Bà's voice called my name.

The next thing I knew, the sound of my life had been restored. I threw up water and my lunch all over the river. My eyes swam with tears, and I was breathing hard. Colours pulsed in front of my eyes.

I was lifted up and I came to on the muddy banks of the river, my clothes ruined.

I slumped down on the weeds. Out of the corner of my eye I saw a little stone shrine for the dead. *That's for me*, I thought.

The old woman had dragged me onto the riverbank. The strength of her wizened body put my own to shame. "Give offerings to that shrine!" she ordered. "The gods were looking out for you!"

My ears were full of water. I spluttered and a boy helped me back to the boat. My friends were white and I was shaking. Pricking my hands on the stems of red roses, I gave my offerings to that small stone shrine in the paddy field by the river.

My breathing was sweet to me, like fragrant flowers. I found myself smiling, though shivering with the cold.

I was restored to life. I had been touched by Quan Âm, the Goddess of Mercy herself.

When I arrived home, lips blue from the cold, wrapped in a tourist T-shirt with the red star emblazoned on it, my parents were aghast.

"I'm lucky!"

I told them of the shrine and how the Goddess of Mercy had saved me. Maybe now I was luckier than my older sister, who was about to be married. Maybe now, since I had almost drowned, my parents would pay more attention to me.

Ma scuttled to the ancestral shrine and lit incense for the ancestors. I bowed with her in front of the faded photo of Bà, who had survived many wars only to die of a stroke during the time of peace.

Bà, I thought, in reverence. It was my grandmother too who had looked out for me in the afterlife, getting the goddess to intercede for me. Bà had always looked after me when I was a little girl, and I was devastated when she died. I knew I was her favourite, much to the chagrin of my older sister. Surely this was proof that the ancestors were looking out for us. My grandmother had been right to hide her Buddhist rituals for so many years during doi moi, when ancestor worship was forbidden. The spirits were more important than the rules of men.

And maybe now I was special too… My sister bought me a bowl of buon bo to eat from the pho seller next door. The spicy beef noodle soup revived me as much as her unexpected kindness.

"Did you ask Quan Âm for a boyfriend?" Father asked. I widened my eyes at him. That had not crossed my mind. She had given me my life. It was enough. I was blessed and no one could take that from me, I thought.

I was so wrong.

That night, next to my sister, I blessed the wooden platform that we slept on. I blessed the warm velvet blanket, the colour of yellow roses, that covered me, blessed the back of my supine, prettier sister, who was about to leave our home. I felt so alive that night, alert to the possibilities.

Hovering on the edge of waking and sleeping, I thanked Quan Âm that I was still alive before receding into a dream. And in my dream, I *was* my sister. I felt the swell of her breasts – larger than mine – in slinky silk clothes, and the gaze of her fiancé upon me. The man that I had only met once in real life, Hieu, had brown, cow-like eyes and slender, milky-white hands. We kissed and he grabbed me. I allowed his hands to roam, and I arched my neck in pleasure…

Then I woke up. Back in my virgin body, sweaty still from my sister's dream. "Did you enjoy West Lake tonight?" I whispered to the air. West Lake was the tryst spot for lovers, and I still felt the tang of moisture on her skin.

My sister sat bolt-upright, yanking the blanket from me. "How did you know? Did one of your friends see us?" she asked urgently. I remained silent in shock and she took my silence for assent.

"Don't you dare tell Ma," she commanded. I shook my head in the near darkness. She lay down again, stiff as the wood we slept on.

I reached out after that dream. I wanted to capture that feeling again, as if cresting on a wave. No man had ever touched me in my own life. I had never had a boyfriend. I wasn't pretty enough.

But it was futile. The feeling eluded me, and I was left with the tantalising memory.

In the morning over breakfast pho my sister watched me like a hawk. We tried not to react to the sound of messaging beeps on her mobile. My parents ate, preoccupied with their food, munching on coriander and bean sprouts. I resolved that day to see more of my parents and not take my family for granted. My close brush with death made me want more from life.

Ma sat on the redwood lounge seat, inlaid with mother-of-pearl, reading the newspaper.

"Ma." I sat down next to her. Ma was so old. For the first time in a while I had the patience to reach out and hold her hand.

"Why this extra attention?" she snapped.

"I have so much to be grateful for," I told her, my mind taking on her preoccupations with the upcoming wedding. How was she going to borrow money so we could go to one of the five-star hotels in town? The invitation list was too long. Who would be left off? And when was the younger daughter going to get a boyfriend?

I let go of Ma's hand, shocked to feel her thoughts, like my sister's thoughts, flooding my mind. Was I reading people's minds?

"I need you to help me prepare for your sister's wedding. You need to be outfitted for being a bridesmaid." She listed what I had already seen in her mind, and I almost expected her to ask me when I was going to have a boyfriend, but she didn't.

"I'm grateful to the goddess and you, Ma," I replied, wanting to share my new joy with her. Maybe I had become psychic like in the stories, when the hero gains magical powers after a brush with death. Ma hmphed and went back to reading the newspaper, leaving me sitting there, stranded in my thoughts.

Then I got up and went to the ancestral shrine. Our great-grandfather stared sternly from his portrait next to my grandmother. The incense was burnt out, so I replaced it, the swirling smoke reminding me of the temple, and I was restored to peace again.

When Father came upstairs, I made the effort to come over and greet him.

When I brushed past his shoulder. I was imprinted with what was on his mind.

"I'll help pay the loan," I offered, helpfully. Father's head snapped to Ma.

"How does she know that?"

Ma's gaze widened. "I didn't tell her! The moneylender I went to was most discreet."

"Shut up! Don't tell her any more! We aren't that badly off…" Father was trying to save face.

Bold with my new gift, I tried again. "Sister wants the best wedding so we won't be ashamed. I will help out."

"How did you know about the loan? If you know, everybody knows," Father said.

"No they don't," I hastened to assure him, and tried to explain. Would they believe me?

"After I nearly drowned, I think something happened to me. Last night I dreamt…" I broke off, not wanting to give away my sister and her secrets. "Anyway, today when you brushed past me I saw what was on your mind! You have to believe me – Ma hasn't told me anything." The words felt strange on my tongue but I hoped Ma and Father would be proud to have such a blessed daughter.

"I haven't," Ma confirmed, staring at me as if she had never seen me before. Then she swore and went to the ancestral shrine. Silence fell upon the room.

Father's eyes narrowed. "Are you telling the truth?" He offered his hand to me. "Tell me what I am thinking."

Reluctantly, I grasped his large hand in mine, slender and white. A psychic could tell fortunes and bring money and luck to the family. They would not need the loan for my sister's wedding. Dutifully, I reported to him what I had sensed in his mind.

"I don't know how you are doing it but it is a gift indeed," he said.

"I am not sure I want everyone to know," I said. This was a gift from the goddess. Was I supposed to make money from it?

"We'll only tell some people. Wealthy ones that can pay," he said, his business mind working. Letting go of his hand, I knew he was lying.

I retreated to my room to ponder what had happened to me. My sister was out working so I had our bed to myself. I curled up under the furry yellow blanket and hugged my legs to my chest. I had never sought to be special, nor had I wanted to read men's minds. But with this new power...

Suddenly tiredness engulfed me. Maybe being psychic had a price.

Liminal light seeped through my eyelids, and I opened my eyes to find myself standing on the shore of a river, much like the river that I had almost drowned in. The light was soft, diffuse, and a familiar voice spoke my name.

I remembered the offerings I had given the shrine then, and tears started in my eyes as Bà appeared, the way she was before she died, in front of me across the river. She was wearing her favourite gold chinois jacket and black pants and her welcoming smile made me feel like a child again. I wanted nothing more than to climb into her arms.

- *Bà, I'm psychic.*
- *I know, child. I can now touch your mind in dreams.*
- *It's a gift from the goddess but Father just wants to make money from it. Is that what psychics are supposed to do?*

Bà laughed.

- *That's my son-in-law. Don't take offence, child. Your parents went through hard times. They save money to pro-tect you.*
- *I know, Bà.*
- *If you can communicate with the dead, you can provide service for the temple. Or you can do what your father says and cater only for his clientele. Your father will make sure that they pay for the privilege.*

I was sixteen years old, almost an adult. Why should I always have to do what Father bid me? He thought that ancestral worship was a superstition. But Bà had proved him wrong.

Father was not always right. This was the first time though that I could do something about it.

- I miss you, Bà.
- I miss you too. Though you now know that I see you
every time you offer incense to me. You are a good
granddaughter.

I smiled at the rare compliment. When I woke up the smile
was still on my face and there was a warm glow inside me.
Indeed, I had been touched.

School the next day was a clamour of noise and chatter. My
best friend, Ngoc, after cursorily asking whether I was all
right, regaled me with the latest gossip from her boyfriend.

"Maybe you can meet him and Nhon after school," she suggested. I inwardly groaned. Nhon made cow eyes at all the
girls and he was not the sort of boy I was looking for. In
fact, I didn't know what I was really looking for, but I did
know what I didn't like in a boy.

I sat through class impatiently. What I really wanted to do
was to try out my new powers.

But I wanted to keep them a secret – especially after seeing
what my family's response had been like. Maybe I could
make people feel better on the sly.

At lunchtime the opportunity came up as our group of
friends sat around the cafeteria with our plates of rice.

"Hi Kim," Dao said as she brushed past me, and I got a
glimpse of her nursing her grandmother, wiping her hot

cheeks with a warm face cloth. My smile must have faded because Ngoc asked me what was wrong.

"I didn't know your grandmother was so sick," I said to Dao. Dao nodded, her face twisting. I put my arm around her and saw flashes of her mother cooking and her father helping out around the house. "Sorry," I apologised as she wiped a tear with her sleeve.

I concentrated on my rice for a little while. Then I looked around my group of friends to decide who to probe next. I cosied up to my best friend and let our shoulders touch.

She was thinking about her boyfriend, in the same way that my sister thought of Hieu. I moved away from her discreetly, trying not to blush.

"What are you thinking about?" I teased.

"The maths test next period," she said. I looked her in the eye, seeing if I could shame her into a confession. But she looked away and ate some rice.

Clearly, my powers made me see what people were thinking rather than what they were saying. I wondered then if I really wanted to know. Maybe I should go to the temple for advice.

Breathing in, I'm aware that I'm breathing in.
Breathing out, I'm aware that I'm breathing out.
Present moment, wonderful moment.

The congregation sat on the floor mats of the meditation hall. The people sitting next to me disturbed me with their heavy breathing. I matched my breath to theirs, breathing mindfully, feeling a smile curl my lips as I settled inside like a ripple calming on a still pool. Inside my mind, pictures bloomed like flowers infused with a soft white light. I saw my sister embracing her lover, her soon-to-be husband. Unnoticed, I saw my parents working hard in the shop below, hawking their wares to tourists that didn't care. Father was counting the money I had given him a few days ago under the watchful eye of my Ma.

I'm prescient! This time the thought did not frighten me. Excited, I opened my eyes in the middle of the meditation hall. Breathing in and out, I felt a surge of compassion for my loved ones. I felt the connectedness of all things and I realised what it meant to inter-be.

Suddenly I was glad I had not drowned in the river. Life was becoming all-important to me now that I was blessed by Quan Âm. Bà was looking out for me, so I had to live. With my new gift, surely one day I would find a husband like my sister and then my parents would be happy with me…

Stretching, I got up at the end of the recitation and padded my way, on stockinged feet, to Quan Âm's shrine. Reaching into my handbag, I took an envelope of spare dong and placed it in the donation box. The large statue of the Goddess smiled serenely down at me. She was white porcelain outlined with gold, her dark eyes painted.

The smell of frangipani from the tree in the courtyard outside tantalised me.

You have given me this gift, I said in my head to the Goddess. *Now I see with eyes of compassion.*

I did not know if I could share my thoughts with the abbot who had preached to us about the ills of young people engaging in sex before marriage. Maybe a nun could tell me what to do.

I padded to the edge of the meditation hall and slipped on my high heels. The evening meal was being served, and the nuns were distributing the food from long benches in the courtyard. The abbess, in her brown robe and skull cap, was talking to petitioners as I approached her. I had always liked the abbess – her eyes were dark and soulful, always with a hint of a smile.

"Sister," I said hesitantly. The abbess turned her attention to me, and her innate wisdom gave me a sense of someone being fully there, a presence. I told her of my near-drowning and the visitation by the goddess. Then I told her of the thoughts I had shared with my family.

"Does this mean I am called to the temple?" I asked. Was this a calling for me to become a nun? I felt so blessed that I would have done anything for the goddess.

The abbess' eyes widened, and I felt her gaze taking in my designer jeans and heels, my make-up bold upon my face. I felt exposed.

"To become a nun is an important step," the abbess told me gently. "You have been blessed by the goddess, but she may have blessed you to show compassion in other ways to those close to you. It has only been a few days, and you are young. To be called to the temple requires much thinking. Are you prepared to give up your material goods and your obligations to your family?"

Humbled by her response, I bowed in gratitude, saying I would need to think more deeply about such things.

My family obligations pulled at me like an undertow. With my sister leaving, I would be the sole carer for my parents. In my haste I had almost forgotten.

Having almost lost the chance to be with them by drowning in the river, was I prepared to let them down now? My work was in the world, for my family and friends.

I made offerings to my grandmother's picture at the family shrine, lighting incense once more. The smoke curled up into the air and the sweet scent brought me back to earth.

I decided I was grateful to my ancestors. My grandmother would not want me to become a nun. She would want me to use my gift for my family.

My sister came home late again. Her eyes were shining as I propped myself up on the wooden platform as she came in. I wanted to tell her of my gift but as soon as she saw me her gaze dropped and she edged around the wooden platform guardedly.

"What's wrong?"

"You're psychic. You don't need me to tell you." Jealousy undercut her voice and it was like a jab to my heart.

"It's not like that… I can't just… I have to hold your hand first…"

"You knew about West Lake. You probably blabbed it to all your friends. I don't want to sleep next to you anymore, but Ma said I'm going to stay here till I'm married."

"Sister… I'm not going to tell anyone your secrets…"

"I don't want you reading my mind."

"Then don't touch me!" Tears sprang to my eyes. I only wanted happiness for my sister but all I got was this hostility.

My sister sat on the edge of the wooden platform, her back towards me. "Don't you dare wreck my wedding. I felt so sorry for you when you almost drowned. Now you just want attention on you instead of me."

I sat up, my mouth open. I was not that small-minded. I wasn't.

"I don't want you to read my mind," she went on. "My mind is the only thing that is private about me."

"That's okay," I said and lay down again. I listened to my sister undress and she snuggled under the blankets we shared. True to her word, she kept a small distance between us so we wouldn't touch. I sank into the small island of my body, curled up cold and alone and muffled my face so she wouldn't hear me crying.

2

That Saturday I received my first customer.

In the morning we had gone to the market and bought crabs for lunch – a special meal for my sister's fiancé, Hieu. I had received little jolts of prescience at the market. My fingers accidently brushed against the fishmonger's palm when I handed her money. It brought a smile to my face – she counted us as her best customers.

I was tempted to touch the hands of a beggar woman on the street, her conical hat upturned for money, but my mother's brisk walk and sister's gaze discouraged me. My sister was still cold towards me, and she avoided touching me, despite the jostling of the market. The crowds were overwhelming, with images of people thinking of market goods and money and occasionally of a loved one, like my mother, eager to impress her soon-to-be son-in-law.

When we reached the open street, I relaxed and sighed.

"Were you seeing things in there?" my sister snapped as we crossed the road to go home.

"Yes," I told her, and saw the pride gleam in my mother's eyes.

At home I chopped up the greens while my mother's and sister's dextrous hands prepared the crab. The maid had cleaned up the house and bought flowers – roses – that scented our house and the shrine.

"You have to show your husband you can cook," my mother said to my sister. When her fiancé arrived, I felt a small echo of what I had felt in my dream. Blushing, I turned away as he came in, dressed in a shirt and jeans. Thankfully my sister did not seem to notice me – she was so captivated by his arrival.

He is not that good-looking, I thought, *in the reality of our house*. But the way my mother and sister behaved towards him, he could have been a god. Even Father came up to greet him and shook his hand vigorously.

"Would you like a beer?" Father asked, and Hieu refused. If it were possible, my sister's regard for him rose even higher.

The maid served the crab and greens. Hieu smiled at my sister, pleased, as with the smacking of lips and the cracking of claws we set to the meal. My fingers grew sticky with the innards of crab, and I washed my hands in the little bowl of lemon water in front of me.

"How is your family business?" Father asked.

"It's going well. We signed an agreement with an exporter today."

"An exporter," Father echoed, nodding at Ma.

"We are going to expand our operations and Tam can work in our company before she has children." Hieu spoke as if my sister wasn't there, but she beamed anyway.

Father sighed, sated, and sat back in his chair. Then he looked at me. I glanced up, disconcerted. I had been ignored the whole meal.

"Fetch us some tea, daughter." I stood up to find the maid. She had already set the teapot and cups on a tray and was boiling the water. When she saw me, her eyes widened. She almost spilt the kettle.

I sighed in exasperation, unwittingly copying my mother. Was everyone going to react this way if they knew I was psychic?

Hands shaking, the maid poured the water into the teapot and then put the kettle down.

"There you are, madam," she said. Before she had resented serving me. Now she was scared of me. I didn't know which I preferred.

I took the tray out to the dining room. My father and mother looked at me proudly as I served the tea to Hieu first. When he took the cup Father suddenly jabbed me with his elbow. The cup spilt all over Hieu's jeans.

"Kim!" scolded my father and my mother, and my sister frowned. Hurriedly I got a dishcloth and dabbed his leg. Unwelcome flashes intruded into my mind. My sister's soft, wet mouth. Nervousness about being with my family. How proud he was of his family and how he hoped he was worthy of my sister's love.

My parents watched me with avid eyes and Ma followed me into the kitchen when I rinsed the dishcloth.

"What did you see?" she hissed, clutching my arm like pincers. Again I saw flashes. She wanted to know everything about Hieu. *Everything.*

"He loves Duong," I said.

"Yes? And what else?"

"He wants to please us. He comes from a good family." As was my practice, I told Ma what she wanted to hear. I tried not to think of West Lake.

"Is he telling the truth about the exporter?"

I nodded. "He's very proud," I said, unwittingly.

She let my arm go. "Good girl," she said, and went to the dining room. I rubbed my arm where she had grasped it and saw the maid watching me.

Annoyed, I stalked back out to the dining room. Ma was smiling and so was Father. The chocolates were being opened and my sister turned her smile to me, then she winked.

Oh!, I thought, my anger at being used turning into joy. It was my sister's idea! Bathing in the warmth of my family's acceptance of my gift, I took a chocolate from her, gratefully.

Hieu smiled too, sensing that he had won us over, and relaxed his shoulders.

We were all so happy…

On Sunday, I went to the temple with my family. Ma bought five different-coloured fruits for the goddess – bright-pink dragon fruit, bananas, apples, mandarins and jack fruit. She also brought some soft drink and chocolates – extra bounty.

I felt the warmth and support of my family like I never had before. For the first time Father approved of me, the unmarried second daughter, and I blossomed in the attention.

My new sense enlivened me, when normally I would have been distracted through the dharma teaching. My skin prickled whenever someone brushed close to me, and I sensed the steady calm of the nuns and monks, walking mindfully among us.

After the dharma talk, we lined up for the communal lunch. I was with my sister and Hieu when Father came up to us with one of his friends. Bác stank of recent cigarette smoke and his eyes darted like sparrows. His gaze, like most men's, dwelled on my sister's beauty before turning to me.

"I hear you tell fortunes," Bác said.

"Get your lunch later," Father ordered. I followed them to a more secluded part of the courtyard. The all-seeing eye of the Buddha was emblazoned in a blue mosaic on the wall behind us as we squatted together on the ground.

"Give her your hand," Father encouraged, and the other man held out a browned palm to me. I looked at Father and he smiled at me as I tentatively shook the man's hand.

I saw the roll of dice, and the fall of mah-jong tiles. Piles of money appearing and disappearing, the suddenness of guilt and the worry of his wife.

"Am I lucky?" he asked me, his eyes peering into mine. I took a breath and glanced at Father out of the corner of my eye.

"You gamble and you think your wife doesn't know," I said, sotto voce. "You've lost money recently. You're not lucky when you gamble."

He abruptly withdrew his hand and looked down at the ground. "I hoped she didn't know. Yet she still hasn't left me…" He glanced at Father.

"I will go home tonight." He gave me a little bow and stood up. Father joined him, and the two men walked a little way. Then I saw him quickly give Father some money before leaving.

I stayed seated on the ground. My heart swelled with this new power I had over people's lives. I could change lives with the goddess watching over me!

Then Father stood over me, his shadow falling onto the wall. "Kim. Come with me to my study group tonight."

I opened my mouth in protest. I was going out with my girlfriends for ice cream. Standing up, I closed my mouth when I saw the serious look in Father's eyes. "We won't need anyone else's help when we have your gift," he said, and I reluctantly obeyed.

Father's study group took place in a bia hoi where the only other women, apart from myself, were the servers. The place reeked of beer and cigarettes, and I sipped at my lukewarm Coke, wishing I was elsewhere.

When Father drank he got loud and embarrassing. Tonight was no exception, and his behaviour was matched by that of his friends.

"So why have you brought along your girl?" one of them finally bothered to ask, after an hour of gossip and complaining about how business was going badly.

"She can tell us our fortunes," Father said.

"Oh yeah? Am I going to get lucky tonight?" one of them leered, and I withdrew further into my shell. I should have been out on my moped tonight, cruising with my girlfriends, but instead here I was, being shown off like a prize cat or dog.

Amid laughter, one of the quieter ones approached me, his hand outstretched. When I was little, he used to be kind to me and my sister, so I took his hand willingly.

Flashes of his family ran past my eyes like a movie. His obedient wife and his wayward son, who was out tonight showing off his new mobile phone. Then glimpses of a Party meeting dominated by old men in suits.

"What can you tell me?" he asked.

"I'd like a new mobile like you gave your son," I said, surprising him. He took a step back with a twinkle in his eye and shook his head.

Father laughed awkwardly and nudged another one of his friends in front of me, a man with hands that sweated like a pig. He was worried about getting a promotion. I was beginning to enjoy the newfound respect the men had for me.

Then another man joined hands with me – a skinny, inoffensive-looking man in a white shirt – and my body was jolted. I pulled my hand away, recoiling. He had hit his wife before coming here and was contemplating giving her a beating when he went home.

"What's wrong?" Father asked.

I gulped and stood up. "He should treat his wife better," I said to guffaws of laughter, and I fled outside the bia hoi hall, shaking.

Out on the street, the whirr of mopeds and the honking around me brought me back to my senses. *That mean man*, I thought. Who would have guessed that the skinniest one of them would terrorise his wife and little children with the lash of a belt?

I wanted to go home and hide, but fear of Father kept me standing outside the bia hoi.

It seemed like forever until Father came out sweating and looking for me.

"You earned us the rest of the loan money," Father said. "Go off and be with your friends."

He patted me on the back. I knew he hadn't told me the whole truth. He had made more money than the loan and was going to use the rest of the money to gamble tonight. Ashamed, I fled, hating myself and hating the men inside.

When I got home my best friend had responded to my call and was waiting for me on her lemon-yellow moped. Tonight she was wearing a tight, frilly red sun-dress and vivid make-up. I clambered up behind her, feeling soiled and filthy.

"Why did you have to go to a bia hoi tonight?" she asked me.

"My father wanted to show me off," I said.

"I thought it was your sister that was getting married…" she said as we headed to the ice cream place at Hoan Kiem Lake.

"Er…" Leaning on her, I sensed that she was looking forward to seeing her boyfriend and she hoped that she wouldn't end up as smelly as me.

"You know when I almost drowned?"

"Yeah?"

"Well, I've become psychic."

"Really?" She slowed down so suddenly that I was thrown forward. She bumped the moped onto the pavement to park.

"It's true," I said. "My father has been using me to make money." I bit my tongue before I could spill out my family shame. Ngoc looked sideways at me.

"So are you going to become an old len dong lady and charge people to see your ceremonies?" she asked. I laughed at her comment. Len dong ladies pretended to be in a trance and covered themselves in a red veil, receiving offerings after hours of ceremony.

We walked into the ice cream shop and got a table overlooking the road towards the lake. Pop music played and I relaxed for the first time that night, ordering coconut, durian and lychee ice cream.

"It's not like that," I said. "When I hold people's hands I can see into their minds."

"Oh!" She pondered for a while, then took a sip of water. "You could tell me whether my boyfriend is serious or not," she suggested lightly.

"Are you sure you want to know?" I blurted, before thinking.

"What do you mean by that?" her pretty face frowned.

"I... it's just that..." I found I couldn't tell her about Father's friends and their upsetting revelations.

She shrugged, looking away from me over to the green calm of the lake. "If you were my best friend and you were really psychic, you'd tell me," she said.

Tears came to my eyes. Sensing she had gone too far, my friend put her arm around me, but underpinning her concern was a feeling of annoyance – she wanted to get rid of me and see her boyfriend.

Thankfully, the ice cream came, breaking off the contact. I was beginning to wonder if the goddess' gift had another side that I had not expected.

The taste of the green durian ice cream restored me a little bit.

"I'm sorry," I said. "It's just that sometimes I see the ugly side of people and I want to think the best of everyone."

She nodded, drinking her strawberry milkshake, although I could see that she didn't understand. "I'm not the best company tonight. Maybe you can drop me off home before you meet up with Tuan."

"Sure," she said, relief in her eyes.

At home everything was quiet. The maid had gone home and Ma was out with her friends. I went up to the ancestral altar and gazed at the statue of Quan Âm, still smiling benignly down at me.

"Why have you given this to me?" I asked the statue. I only wanted everyone in my life to be happy, including me.

3

The next day after school I came home to find a wrapped present for me on the bed. Inside, I found a mobile phone just like the one Father's friend had given his son. Involuntarily, I smiled. My faith in the goodness of my family was being restored.

I did not touch anyone that day. Dinner was quiet, just Ma and me. Ma said she was happier and was relieved that my sister's wedding planning was going well.

Then the following day Father brought his friend and another man I did not know home for dinner. Ma apologised that she was not ready for them and sent the maid out to get more food.

My new mobile secure in my pocket, I smiled graciously to Father and the friend who had indirectly suggested it to me.

"This is Phuc," Father introduced and nodded at the other man. "You can take her hand," Father encouraged.

"Hello Bác Phuc," I said, bracing myself even before touching his hand. And when I did, I gasped. The man was high up in the Communist Party and had come especially to see me. "I'm honoured to meet you," I said politely, masking my apprehension at the images that were in his mind.

Ma served some wine for the guests, and we sat on the red-wood furniture. It became clear to me that my mother and father already knew who this man was.

What did he want to do with me?

"Congratulations on your daughter's upcoming nuptials," Bác Phuc said. "You are lucky to have such beautiful daughters." He turned to me.

"Do you know why I have come to see you today?" he asked me directly.

"You are from the government," I said nervously. "You want me to work in an office."

He laughed. "Not just any office – the government psychic unit. To assist the state in restoring the honour of the dead."

"I thought…" and I bit my tongue. My family were only acquaintances of a Party member – we were not well connected. Not connected enough to win a government posting.

Bác Phuc continued. "We need genuine psychics to help us. Do you understand?"

I nodded vigorously, and found my father and mother staring at Bác Phuc with astounded eyes.

"You can work with the Bureau. Your pay will be more than adequate." He smiled. His teeth were white and even.

"You need psychics that badly?" asked Father, trying to take advantage of the situation.

"There is a long waiting list for our services," Bác Phuc said. I opened my mouth to protest and then shut it again. "Of course you will get leave for your sister's wedding," he said, as if reading my mind, and I realised with a shiver that Bác Phuc might be psychic too.

At that moment the maid came in with the banh cuon, white vermicelli with prawns, from a restaurant close by.

"I will come and collect you. I won't stay for dinner," Bác Phuc said. "You can stay," he ordered Father's friend, who nodded.

"Thank you for coming to our home," Father said automatically, and we nodded, too stunned to speak. Bác Phuc stood up, his wine untouched, and Father walked him down the stairs.

Ma stared at me with frightened eyes and came over and hugged me close. "You told them, didn't you," she accused Father's friend.

"I didn't." He spread his hands helplessly. "They already knew."

I was dreading the next day when I found out Father had set up a celebratory dinner. I could not look those men and their wives in the eye. I felt like a freak on display.

Ma bought a roast pig to celebrate. I could not hide in my room all evening, so when I came out I did so gloved and ready.

Father was already half-drunk and seemed unaware of the unease that hung around his friends. Their wives were already rising to their feet, eyes shining, wanting their fortunes told.

"I'm sorry, but I have to go to work tomorrow," I told them. "Psychic work leaves me exhausted. I have to save my powers for the government."

It was half a lie, half a truth. To my surprise, it worked, although I could see their disappointment. I could not look in the face of the woman who I knew had been beaten. If I did, I fancied she would see the knowledge of her shame on my face.

"My special girl," Father beamed, and I caught my sister staring at me through narrowed eyes. She was jealous again. I was learning to resign myself to it. Once it had been me watching her dates, wondering when it would be my turn. Now it was my turn, but it had become sour. I did not want to work for the government.

The fatty pig sat heavy in my stomach, and I wished I could have had a sip of alcohol. It seemed to make men happy, and it seemed that happiness had eluded my grasp.

The next morning I wore Ma's lilac business suit. It was tight and made me feel awkward.

Father had a headache from the night before and I thought it served him right. I was sipping a glass of filtered coffee with condensed milk after morning pho when Bác Phuc arrived. He nodded at my lilac suit approvingly and refused Ma's offer of coffee. Leaving my half-empty glass behind, I followed him downstairs to his waiting moped.

I sat behind him, crossing my legs, holding onto his waist with gloved hands. He did not comment on the gloves and did not talk to me at all during the short moped trip. We approached a military barracks. He saluted to the armed guard in khaki uniform at the gate and drove in. Behind us, the gates closed, and a hand clenched around my heart.

I knew what an office looked like, but this was not an office. Had he deliberately misled me?

Bác Phuc parked his moped in a line of lookalikes. He curtly gestured for me to follow him. The *tap-tap* of my heels on the concrete echoed in the silent barracks. A brown bird started to sing in the trees above as we headed towards a building flying the star flag. There were no other people in sight, except for the occasional uniformed guard, always male.

The light dimmed as we entered a building. Flickering fluorescent lights lit the stairwell that we ascended. Then we emerged into a corridor with white tiles. Wooden doors lined the corridor. Without hesitation, Bác Phuc opened a door and gestured for me to come in.

Inside was the office I had seen in his mind. There was a large table in the centre of the room covered with a topographical map. On one side was a desk, Bác Phuc's desk, the wall behind it covered with memos and a framed degree of some sort. On the other side were a couple of chairs, a small table for meetings and a large bookcase. The books were in Vietnamese, French, English and Russian.

"Sit down," Bác Phuc said. "We'll wait for the others to arrive."

I sat on a chair and looked at the map. It marked out a large, dotted road with land subdivisions faintly visible. Chua Huong, a temple, was labelled on the top of one hill.

There were clusters of Xs around the temple and rectangles that could have been houses.

"What do you make of it?" Bác Phuc asked in my ear. He was standing too close and I could smell his aftershave.

"Where is it?" I asked.

"Just out of Huế. Do you know what the Xs are?" he queried.

"Graves?" I guessed.

"Bodies."

The door of the office opened, and Bác Phuc stiffened. Instinctively, I stood up. An older man in a military uniform came in, accompanied by an aide carrying an archive box.

"So this is the new one," he said to Bác Phuc.

Bác Phuc nodded.

"Sit," he ordered, and we gathered around the map. The aide put the archive box down on the table. His fingers were long and slender, not muscled like Bác Phuc's and the military officer's. I guessed he was a secretary.

"First, a test."

The aide opened the archive box and the smell of mould reached me. He handed the box to Bác Phuc.

"We need to know if you can divine this," Bác Phuc said to me gently, almost apologetically, as he presented the box to me.

Reeling slightly, I looked into the box of earth at the shards of bones lying on top. I pulled off my right glove, grimacing at what they were asking me to do. I glanced up at Bác Phuc, who nodded encouragingly at me.

I put my hand in the box and touched the bone. It was dry and splintery. Then I was overwhelmed by images.

Bang! Crash! An explosion of white light. Screaming. Fire. Then a drawn-out wail.

"Ma!" I screamed and jerked my hand out of the box.

No one else moved. Bác Phuc shut the box. The officer looked at me closely.

"What did you see?" he demanded.

"An explosion. A fire. He is a ghost. He died far from home. No one… no one… pays respects…"

I began to shake. My mind was filled with a white light. Someone put his hand on my shoulder.

"No one pays respects to me." The voice from my throat was not my own.

Bác Phuc's voice came from above me. "Who are you?"

"Nguyen Dung. From Huế. No one respects me."

"We will find your family. We will reunite your remains and they will pay respects to you."

The white light disappeared as suddenly as it had appeared. I opened my eyes to find myself on the floor. Bác Phuc was handing me a glass of water. I sat up, self-consciously crossing my legs in front of the three men. "What happened?" I asked.

"We'll send you both to Huế tomorrow," the officer said. "Take care of it."

Bác Phuc took my elbow and helped me to my feet. He gave me back my glove and, shivering, I put it on. The aide retrieved the box from the table and he and the officer left the room.

Bác Phuc peered into my face. "Kim, are you there?"

"Of course I am," I snapped, indignant at the way I was being treated. The officer had acted as if I hadn't even been there.

He sat me down on the chair and took a seat opposite me.

"We are going to Huế to help with the excavation of a mass grave. The roadworks crew uncovered it while building the new highway and no one will work there until the graves are removed."

"I don't want to go to Huế," I said. The backwater of the old imperial capital was the last place I wished to end up.

"You will be back for your sister's wedding, I promise you. We will pay for everything for you and even give you some pocket money of your own to spend. The tailors there are cheaper than in Hanoi."

His kindness made me feel ungrateful, even though it was patronising. I had never been out of Hanoi.

He took a folder, with my name on it, from his desk.

"We have to sign some paperwork before you go."

Looking at the lengthy contract, I gasped at the large amount I was being paid. My parents would never have to borrow money again. I signed on the dotted line.

Bác Phuc took me home for lunch.

"Spend the rest of the day packing and saying your good-byes. We'll pick you up in the morning at six." He nodded to me as I gingerly got off his moped and headed upstairs.

Ma was sitting at the table counting money. When she saw me she started, clearly surprised.

"You are home for lunch? I wasn't expecting …"

"It's okay, Ma," I told her, sitting down at the table. "They've given me the rest of the day off. Tomorrow they are sending me to Huế with Bác Phuc. They want me to identify some war dead…" I choked on the words. Unwillingly, I flashed back to the wrench of physical pain that had thrown me out of my chair with the explosion.

"War dead? That's all in the past. They want to dig up more of that?" Ma asked.

"They found a mass grave when they were building the highway. The site is haunted, and no one will work there until the graves are exhumed."

Ma swallowed and glanced towards the family shrine. "Quan Âm will look after you," she told me, patting my gloved hand.

"I'm being paid, too… Sister's wedding will be taken care of."

Ma smiled at me gratefully and the warmth replaced the trepidation I had felt since leaving the military barracks.

She put rubber bands around the hundred-thousand dong notes on the table and packed the money away, still smiling. I had not seen her so happy with me for a long time.

"Is Bác Phuc married?" she asked.

"I don't know," I answered, surprised.

"He is high up in the Party," Ma murmured to me, and I realised where her thoughts were headed.

"Don't fail on your first assignment," she told me severely, before going to the kitchen and ordering the maid to get us lunch.

I sat at the table looking down at my white-gloved hands. Ma had not even asked me when I was coming back.

Packing and the thought of flying in a plane began to excite me a little. It was like a fairy tale, being whisked away by Bác Phuc to a glorious future with the Party.

Except for the dead. I shivered as I folded my jeans into a suitcase borrowed from the neighbours. Was this what the goddess intended for me? That I would work for the government? Reuniting the remains of the dead with their descendants was important, worthwhile work, I told myself. But the bloodiness of that vocation reeked to me.

I was born after the Fall of Saigon. The war was something preserved in museums, which haunted the generation before mine. At sixteen I was supposed to be free of the ties of history. I was going to get married like my sister and live in a large apartment with my husband.

Now that future seemed impossible. I changed out of the suit and tried to pack it away. I was told to wear clothes that could get dirty. Bác Phuc was going to take me to the excavation site, and I was going to work from four in the morning and stop at eleven, when it would get too hot.

He said I could fly back for my sister's wedding if we had finished the work. So, my suspicions were right – Bác Phuc was going to work with me. He, too, was a psychic.

I sat on the bed pondering Ma's words. Bác Phuc had been kind to me. And no one would want to marry a psychic who could ferret out all their secrets – except maybe another psychic who could understand.

4

The plane whirred and I breathed in the cold, too-thin air. I did not realise I was grasping the armrests until Bác Phuc told me to relax.

"You haven't flown before," he said.

"No. Sorry." I took a warm hand towel from the hostess and wiped my face with it.

Bác Phuc had no rings on his fingers, and I wanted to please him. For the plane ride I had worn my most flattering tight white blouse with my jeans and good black high heels. I saved my sneakers in my luggage for when we got to the excavation site.

"How long have you worked for the Bureau?" I boldly asked as we waited for take-off.

"Three years," he replied. "Do you have a boyfriend?" he asked me in return.

"No." I smiled and shook my head.

"You will find it's hard for others to understand."

The words clattered as truth into my consciousness. My sister had not hidden her relief that I was leaving for Huế. She was the only one who asked if I was coming back for her wedding.

"Your family aren't members of the Party?" Bác Phuc continued.

"No." I wondered why he'd asked. Surely he would know?

"When we come back, I'll take you to a Party meeting as a guest," he said.

"Thank you." I knew I was supposed to be grateful but in my new cynicism I wondered if I would be asked to perform like a trained dog for them the way I had been put on display for the military officer.

I observed Bác Phuc out of the corner of my eye while he read the airline magazine. His skin was civilian white, yet his chest was broad – he had done military service, I sensed, evident in his walk and the fatigue lines at the edges of his eyes. He was maybe ten years older than me.

"How did you become a psychic?" I asked when drinks were served.

"I came close to death," he said, and his eyes closed for a moment. Then he opened them again.

"I nearly drowned," I said, my words tumbling out of my mouth. "On the way to the Perfume Pagoda."

"You're very lucky," he told me, and a blossom of rapport bloomed in my breast. He was the first to put into words how I thought of what had happened to me. I could not help but smile as I looked out of the window at the clouds we were flying above. The sky was a hopeful blue, the white clouds undulated like the sea.

We touched down in Huế and I was struck by the provinciality of the airport, with its single airstrip and only our plane on the tarmac. We were greeted by a man in a khaki uniform who held Phuc Le's name up on a sign. He grabbed our luggage, escorting us to a black government car.

I was dumbstruck by the way I was treated as deferentially as Bác Phuc, a total contrast to the military officer's earlier assessment of me. As we drove to what passed for the city's centre, I looked out onto the green rice paddies and the bicycles and mopeds flowing past. The Perfume River was a startling green, lined with a park with Communist block-shaped sculptures. Dragon boats lined up at the waterfront waiting for tourists. Already the day was uncomfortably warm and cyclo drivers dozed in the cabs of their vehicles, lined up opposite the hotels.

This time I was not surprised when the car pulled up to the biggest hotel by the riverfront.

Uniformed men opened the doors and I stepped out temporarily into the sweltering heat of the late morning. Bác Phuc led the way into the ornate lobby, with gold-rimmed clocks showing the local time in major cities of the world. Girls my age in tight red áo dài were attending to the phones and the guests.

One looked askance at me in my tight jeans and high heels as I accompanied Bác Phuc but stopped when she saw our documentation and travel passes. "Sir. Madam," she nodded to us both.

"Have a rest," Bác Phuc told me. "The cool change comes at about three here. Our driver will take you anywhere you want to go. I'll see you at dinner about six." With that, he led me to the elevator and handed me my room key.

His room was next door to mine and the bellboy opened the door. I wandered in and let the bellboy put the key in the slot to demonstrate how to turn on the air-conditioner and the lighting. I followed him further in as he showed me the opulent bathroom, nodding as if it were commonplace, and let him out the door, trying to hide my excitement.

I had my own bedroom! The double-size bed – all to myself – seemed enormous to me, as was the TV, hidden in a wooden cabinet. The room was large enough for a sitting table and two chairs as well as a desk.

I was alone. I sat down on the bed, which was soft to the touch. I peeled off my gloves one at a time to free my sweating hands, just as a knock on the door revealed the bellboy again with my suitcase. He put it near the desk and exited. I did not dare rise nor tip him with my fingers bare.

I jumped off the bed and opened the curtains. The window overlooked the river. In the distance I could see a road bridge. I put my hands to the glass and left sweaty palm marks. So this was Huế. It seemed rural compared to Hanoi.

I changed into my pyjamas for the midday nap and curled up in the middle of the bed. It was empty and suddenly I missed my sister's back to lean on, and her breathing, which tells me I am not alone. When I returned home after the wedding, I would have that room to myself. My life would be like this.

Loneliness yawned within me. I had told my best friend over the phone I was being sent to Huế but she had been more interested in telling me about the latest goings-on with her boyfriend. Everyone was tied up in their own lives and too busy to listen to me.

No one in my life cared about war graves or the dead. They were too concerned with the living.

I was awake and dressed at four the next morning when the driver knocked on my door.

Huế was just beginning to wake up. The pho sellers were assembling their wares and the roads were almost empty. The dawn was mild, and I was grateful for the thermos of tea that the driver thoughtfully provided us with.

It only took ten minutes of driving for us to reach the countryside beyond Huế. Trees and greenery dominated, and chickens ran across the road. I spotted a turn-off for Chua Huong and knew we were close.

We came across the new highway suddenly, in an open clearing. The road was newly asphalted and came to a halt at a large roped-off pit. Already two labourers were standing around smoking. The driver parked and we got out, catching a glimpse of the pink dawn edging over the horizon.

Bác Phuc approached the workmen, who straightened up and only surreptitiously glanced at me.

"Are the novices from the temple here yet?"

One of the workmen shrugged. Bác Phuc gestured to me.

"Come have a look." He didn't have to tell me to not touch anything. "The geomancer tells me that the discoloured soil here is decomposed bodies."

I glanced into the pit. Mud and water oozed, and I glimpsed shards of bone embedded in the sides of the pit.

"Mass grave. Why did you bring a woman out here?" one of the workmen said.

"She's a psychic. She's part of the reburial team."

The workmen's eyes widened. Then they nodded in understanding as the sound of a moped cut into the quiet of the dawn. Pulling up at the site was a brown-robed abbot and a novice robed in grey. The novice was holding onto ceramic pots, precariously bundled together, for the remains of the bones.

I bowed to the abbot, who smiled at me and Bác Phuc.

"Thank you for coming," he said to us gently. "These disturbed souls have been troubling us greatly. We have been waiting for you."

The novice set up incense on a little mound away from the pit.

"I can assist you in finding the descendants of these men and women if they are from around here," the abbot said.

The workmen holding small hand shovels bowed to the abbot, then jumped into the pit. Too soon, I was presented with a shovel full of mud and earth from which shards of bone were poking. I took off my gloves and gingerly reached out to touch the protruding fragments.

A scream. A bolt of pain lanced through my insides. Then wailing. She had been abandoned, defiled, and murdered. Her family could not find her. They had offered outdoor offerings to the lost souls but could not honour her at the altar.

"She lived in the village not far from here. She was killed by Americans." I could not bring myself to say what had happened to her before her death. So I began describing the scenery around the village, the hills that backed onto her family's farm and the closeness of Chua Huong. She had had three brothers and two sisters.

The abbot listened gravely to my babbling, then produced a notebook from a bag by his side. "I think I know which family this is," he said and motioned for the novice to bring over one of the reburial urns. The remains were put in the jar and the abbot murmured some instructions to the novice.

Bác Phuc watched approvingly and smiled at me for the first time. Putting a hand over my stomach from the phantom pains, I tried to smile back, but instead found myself fighting tears.

Bác Phuc came over to my side with the thermos of tea. "Have a rest for a few minutes my dear," he said.

Clumsily, I walked away from the pit and sat on the car bonnet. I crossed my arms, hiding my head in my hands to conceal my shame from the men.

The hours passed by in a blur. I was hit by the pain and humiliation of death again and again. Bác Phuc began to work alongside me, his face stoic. He would squat down next to the remains, his face a frown, and close his eyes. Then he would tell the abbot what he saw.

With the help of the abbot we were able to identify nine people from nearby villages. Then I was presented with another mound of mud with bones protruding from the muck. I was reminded of the bones of a chicken after the slaughter as I braced myself for the impact of touching them.

The shock comes like a pistol shot to the back of the head. I am drenched in fear, standing in line, waiting. Ma stands next to me, clutching my hand, sweating. I had been told to be quiet, and this time none of my cheekiness asserts itself. Even the adults are quietly standing in the darkness down in the basement of the school.

Then a door opens and men in black come down the stairs with pistols. With frightening efficiency they make us kneel on the concrete floor. A gun muzzle glints in the dim light, and then a crack. My teacher Long falls forward. Someone screams.

Panic… and Ma cowers to the ground, covering me with her body. More cracks and the smell of blood. Then a thunder-clap in my ear. Ma goes limp above me and I am squashed under her weight. I wriggle and blinding pain shoots up my leg. Then I fall…

A child! The National Liberation Front had murdered families in cold blood, just like the Americans and the Army of the Republic of Việt Nam had. I recoiled from the knowledge. Opening my eyes, I saw Bác Phuc looking at me with concern.

"A child…" I stammered.

"Where did they come from?" Bác Phuc asked, his stare fixed to my face.

"South." The word was shaken out of me.

"I see." Bác Phuc gestured at the workmen and the area of mud that the geomancer indicated was dug up and thrown to the side of the road. The abbot knelt by my side, and I turned to him.

"They aren't honouring the dead…"

The abbot looked at me with large, sorrowful brown eyes. "These are Southern dead. Your colleagues are from the government."

A chill ran down my spine as I realised the political implications of what I had seen.

"They will still haunt the road…" I murmured.

The abbot paused for a moment, then looked away. "In the eyes of the Buddha there are no political sides or ideology. We will look after them." He rose to his feet suddenly and Bác Phuc approached, indicating I should get back to work.

Fucking gooks. Never let a man sleep. Have to get out of this hellhole, stay alive for three more days then out of here. Never again.

"American," I said. I wanted to sit down and cry and never get up again. The workmen heaped the soil and remains on the side of the road. The novice went away on his moped and came back with wooden boxes lined with red paper. The American remains were placed in the boxes and put in the back of our car.

"The Americans like it when we can return remains to them," Bác Phuc said neutrally. The labourers returned to work and Bác Phuc clambered back into the pit.

Exhausted and covered with mud, I sat down on the side of the road. I imagined I was covered with the bloody remains of the victims I had seen. Even the American was treated with more respect than the Southern Vietnamese. It made no sense. Surely the souls from the South would haunt the road too?

Shivering, I unwillingly flashed to what I had seen of the American's feelings. He had died slowly, suffering the same way our people had.

"We will pray for them," the abbot said softly in my ear. I turned to the wise man standing impassively by my side. The novice had lit more incense and begun a quiet chant a few steps away from the open grave site. The sun had risen, and the heat of the day was making itself felt. I glanced at Bác Phuc but his eyes were closed in trance, talking to the geomancer about what he saw.

"Politics keep men divided," the abbot said. "But we all suffer, no matter which side we are on. After we die there are no distinctions. You are not like him. Your spirit is still young. If you need counsel, please come to Chua Huong and ask for me." The abbot left my side as if he had said nothing of import and returned to the pit.

Bác Phuc had identified more Southern soldiers and the heap by the side of the road grew. I sipped a cup of tea, listening to the chant for the dead and then the sound of the bell from the novice. The ringing returned me to memories of my own temple in Hanoi. A moment of peace came over me.

Then I began to cry for what I had lost.

5

At the hotel I stripped off my muddy clothes and stood in the shower for a long time. The sound and feel of the hot water running over my body washed away the stench of death and the agony of the ghosts. Then I lay down on the big bed wishing for sleep and forgetfulness, but I was unable to nap. Would the ghosts haunt me in my sleep? How much more did we have to do?

I felt like I was drowning again. I decided to find some lunch and wandered down to the reception area.

Bác Phuc was there with his driver.

"Would you like to have some lunch?" he asked. I was so weary I did not even pick up the convenient nature of the meeting.

The driver took us to a banh cuon place. Bác Phuc was dressed in jeans and a shirt, the most casual clothing I had ever seen him in. He wore sunglasses, so I could not read his eyes.

The driver sat in the car while we went inside the cafe and crouched down on baby plastic chairs. Plates of soft white vermicelli with pork mince were placed in front of us.

"How are you feeling?" Bác Phuc asked, and I nearly cried again at his kindness. "The first day is always the worst," he told me. "It gets easier."

I found myself choking on the banh cuon, though my stomach welcomed the food. "How much do we have to do?" I asked, hating how it came out more like a plaintive wail than a casual enquiry.

"We did thirty bodies today. I don't know how big the graves are around here. There are so many missing… We only have to do enough to clear the way for the road." I stared at him. "The locals would have us live here forever if they could. But our instructions are clear. We are only here for three days. Then they can excavate the bones and send them to Hanoi for us to identify what we can."

"Why didn't they just…"

"We had to come here to demonstrate that we are able to do what we do. The abbot and the workers will spread the word around." He turned his attention back to eating.

"How do you cope?"

He looked at me. "I did military service. I tell myself they are only pictures, things that happened to other men. I'm still alive – it did not happen to me."

I swallowed and reached for a cup of tea. I didn't know what to say.

"You are very lucky and young. You'll get over it," he told me. I thought of the money I was earning. It had to be enough to keep me going through all the flashbacks. It had to.

That afternoon, even the fitting of my new tailored suit did not lift my spirits. Even though I got a bargain, I still hated Huế and wanted to go home. When I returned to the hotel I found a red cellophane-wrapped box and flowers on the side-table, an arrangement of red roses and white carnations whose scent filled the room.

The novice had run the present and flowers down to us at the hotel. They left me in my room to open the present, a box of chocolates with an envelope. Inside the envelope were one hundred American dollars and a note.

Thank you for restoring our daughter to us.

I put the envelope down on the box and sat on the bed. For the first time that day I felt that I had done something worthwhile.

That night after dinner, I found myself exhausted. Sleep grasped me and sucked me down into unconsciousness.

She was willowy and thin, her muscles hard from peasant work. She wore a conical hat, a simple blouse, and trousers. She was carrying a rifle as she walked towards me over a paddy field backed by a mountain. The colours were soft, a liminal grey.

- *Miss Kim, psychic.*

She mouthed the words and I bowed to her. I was wearing the áo dài that I was going to wear to my sister's wedding – burgundy with flowers.

- You cannot ignore us.
- I'm not ignoring you. I am doing my best to find your families.
- We fought for our country too. I'm young, like you. I died under fire. I forgive you working for the Communists. You cannot help that. But you must help us.

I realised then that she had fought for the South. Behind her I saw the grey silhouettes of other soldiers. They were waving to us, men and women.

- You are compassionate, blessed by Quan Âm. You know of our suffering. You can help us. Please.

She clasped her hands over my bare fingers. The spiritual contact was softer than the jarring encounters I was getting used to. I saw pictures of her family and her lover, whom she had not seen for thirty-five years. In her mind she had been beautiful and blessed until the village was taken over by the Communists. Then I saw a familiar face. It was the abbot I'd met that day, but with hair pulled back, in the robe of a novice monk.

- You are blessed by the goddess. You will know what to do when you find me. My name is Thinh.

She smiled and I heard the sound of a bell tolling in the hills. Then the peasant girl faded along with the other soldiers.

I woke up tasting salt in my mouth. The darkness of the hotel room was complete. Someone was knocking at the door.

Startled, I looked at the clock. Four am – I had not set the alarm.

"Coming!" I yelled through the door, and hurriedly changed back into my soiled clothes.

When I saw Bác Phuc I looked at him with wary eyes. He seemed tired and resigned.

Had he had a similar dream? Had my dream been sent by the goddess?

This time when we arrived the abbot and his novice were already waiting for us. More construction workers were there, along with a couple of curious children with their mothers in tow. Word had indeed got around.

Suddenly self-conscious, I stepped up to the lip of the pit. I gazed at the abbot, who nodded at me with eyes dark like lacquer. The first spade of remains was presented to me and, bracing myself, I touched the fragment of bone.

I was jolted into the consciousness of an old man who had died. As I told the abbot of his descendants, I wondered whether my dream had been a true visitation. What would I do if I unearthed Southerners? Would I leave them by the side of the road?

I remembered the words of the abbot. *The goddess forgives and sees all.* There were no politics on the other shore. We were all human on the other shore.

I came across Thinh a few hours later. When my fingers touched the discoloured soil she spoke in my mind with a smile.

- You have found me. My descendants have been searching for me for a long time.

The abbot was waiting for my information when I opened my eyes. Uncertain, I described where she had been killed and where she had lived. The abbot nodded.

"I know the family," he said, gesturing to the novice to come with the ceramic urn for her remains. *How did he know?* I wondered.

Bác Phuc was talking to the geomancer, smoking a cigarette. I did not dare breathe in case I betrayed her, and eagerly reached for the shards of bone in the next shovelful. Another Southerner. And another.

Bác Phuc was identifying them too, and throwing them aside. Was he going to realise that the bones I had identified were also Southern? What would they do to me if my deception was discovered?

To my relief the next bones I identified were of an American. My fingers trembled at the tension in my mind. I felt the build-up of a headache behind my eyes. I had to trust the goddess. She had given me her gift and I had to use it as she saw fit.

The novice came over with a flask of tea. Gratefully, I drank some and sat down on the grass beside the pit as a moped drew up with a man and woman on it. They wore their best clothing, clean pants and shirts, their faces brown and worn by the sun. They headed straight for the abbot and bowed to him. Then the abbot pointed at me.

The three of them came over and I stood up self-consciously, messy.

"This is Kim, the psychic from Hanoi who identified your uncle."

The man smiled and the woman's eyes shone with tears.

"We do not know how to thank you," the man said. He turned to Bác Phuc. "Thank you, Bác," he said, knowing where the real power lay.

"Your uncle sacrificed himself for the greater good," Bác Phuc said. "We have unearthed many heroes here and will build a monument for them beside the highway."

"Thank you, thank you, thank you," the woman said, clutching at me. I drew my hands away from her quickly and she stumbled.

"Miss Kim feels things through her fingers," the abbot explained.

"Sorry, sorry." The woman smiled through her tears. I smiled back, uncomfortable in their gratitude. How would they feel if they knew I was reuniting their former enemy with their families as well? Would I be a traitor in their eyes?

Around the pit a crowd was gathering to watch Bác Phuc. The couple went to join them and I sat down again.

The abbot gestured to the urn that held the remains of the ghost that had visited me. "Would you like to visit the family?" he asked.

Automatically I shook my head. I could not get any more involved than I had already.

"I understand." The abbot breathed in and out. The air smelt of the incense the novice had lit and the fragrance of roses which some of the crowd had brought.

"Buddhists have compassion for all suffering," he said. "You are a good Buddhist." The abbot left my side. I was speechless. He *knew*.

The woman who had thanked me earlier was standing with the crowd. She offered me some cake. Putting on my gloves, I accepted the gift and bowed to her. I felt the crowd's eyes on me. Did they all know? There could be relatives of the Southern dead in the crowd – without touching them, I could not know.

They skirted around the mound of Southerner remains and prayed at the incense, leaving fruit and flowers by the side of the road.

Meanwhile, a taxi pulled up and two women got out. From the way they walked and their clothing I knew they were Việt Kiều, overseas Vietnamese, even before the older one spoke to me.

"This is Thuy, my daughter," she said.

Removing one of my gloves, I touched the younger one's fingers and was not surprised to match her with an executed man, Nguyen, whose remains were heaped in a pile next to the ditch. Touching his remains had made me recoil as my fingers brushed the shot through the back of his head. Now, as I touched the Việt Kiều's fingers, I felt her recoil from me and the force of my reading. The abbot interceded for them, and they bowed to me.

The older Việt Kiều pressed a lucky envelope in my hand, then gave a gift to Bác Phuc. I did not have to look inside the red envelope to know the bribe far exceeded the gifts locals would give.

So it was money that made Bác Phuc honour the Southern dead, and, even then, only to those who could afford it. Disillusioned, I saw him through different eyes. He could be bribed, like all men. *Just like Father*, I thought, with newfound cynicism.

On the way back from the pit at midday, Bác Phuc munched on some sweets given to us by the crowd. I had received flowers and red money envelopes that I had not opened.

"It will be a circus tomorrow," he commented. "The people will ask you to do many things for them," he warned me. "Remember what you have been instructed to do. That's all you do, and no more. People have to realise that our gifts are not free. They can make appointments to see us in Hanoi for personal consultations."

I swallowed and nodded. I wondered whether he included the spirits that visited me at night in his reference to "people."

As we neared the hotel, he suddenly grasped my gloved hand. Instinctively, I blocked my mind, thinking only of a shower and my waiting bed.

"It is tempting to do more and accept everything that is offered to us," he said, looking into my eyes. "But we report to the military about our activities. They keep the Bureau funded for the missing heroes."

He let go of my hand as the car drew up to the hotel entrance. I stepped out of the car and fled to the safety of my room. I had forgotten about the military officer that Bác Phuc reported to. The Party knew my family. We could be promoted or demoted by my actions.

In the air-conditioning of my sterile room my head suddenly hurt. Responsibility cascaded onto me. I knew too much.

I could not betray my family's interests. But the ghosts…

As I lay down on the bed a migraine bloomed behind my eyes, and I sank into darkness.

6

This time Thinh, the peasant girl, smiled at me from under her conical hat. The paddy was a pale green, the sky lighter. The ghosts were holding hands behind her, gazing at me with hopeful eyes.

- *I have spoken with some of the other spirits. They are looking forward to being reunited with their families.*

Feeling awkward in my áo dài, I bowed to the peasant girl and the other spirits gathered around her. They surrounded me and touched me in awe with their ethereal cold fingers. Their voices chorused in my mind: *Miss Kim, Miss Kim!*

One of them wore the black pyjamas of the National Liberation Front. He was eager to touch my hand and did not mind the Southern ghosts flitting by his side. On my tongue was a question about the remains on the side of the road.

- *My abbot will take care of them,* said a female voice in my ear. *In death there are no sides. We are all united on the other shore.*

A bell tolled in the background, ringing through the hollow of my soul. The ghosts faded.

I woke up with the taste of salt in my mouth, my head groggy. It was only three o'clock in the afternoon. I went over to the window and looked out onto the Perfume

River. The cool change would have come by now. I found myself shaking slightly. The spirits had spoken to me and given me a higher purpose than politics. What would my ancestors think?

You know, an unbidden voice rose from the depths of my mind. My grandmother had been a devout Buddhist. She would follow the advice of the spirits.

But what about Bác Phuc's warnings?

I washed my face, touching my skin with my bare hands. I remembered the abbot's invitation to see him. I changed into my jeans and high heels, and tucked my mobile phone into my pocket. I cautiously rode the lift down and to my relief saw no one in the lobby. I felt like a child sneaking away from a parent.

After telling reception that I was going for a walk in the park, I went out the front of the hotel and flagged down a moped. A young boy pulled over and we argued a price for taking me to the temple.

Seeing the hotel recede behind us as the moped gathered speed and the wind whipped through my hair made me feel free of the omnipresent Party. In my memory, unbidden, was the image of my grandmother carrying out ceremonies inside the house when I was much younger. My parents participated but I was to tell no one of what we were doing. When I asked them why we hid, my grandmother told me that the spirits and ancestors were to be honoured no matter what the Party said. The Party was only made up of men.

Father, with a curl of his lip, disapproved. "Stupid superstition," I heard him mutter to Ma when my grandmother was out of sight. But now, after doi moi and into the new century, we were able to worship openly again. My grandmother had been right – to disobey the spirits was to go to hell. They could haunt me in my sleep. Bác Phuc could not reach me in my dreams. At least, I thought he could not.

So much waste, so much sacrifice in war...

As if sensing I was there, the abbot came out of the meditation hall, walking mindfully towards me. In his element, I sensed his universal calm, like the abbess in Hanoi.

"Sister." He bowed to me, and I bowed back. "Come and meet the descendants of some of those you united today. They are paying their respects." This time I could not refuse and followed him into the courtyard. He gestured at a grey-robed novice who, after some brief instructions, hurried away.

"Your minder is not with you," the abbot said.

"No. He does not know I'm here."

"He will come to know, however. Are you prepared to deceive him?"

I swallowed. I had not thought that far ahead.

"Bác Phuc bends the Party rules for his own needs. He may overlook this," the abbot told me. "Which temple do you attend in Hanoi?"

"Green Willow," I said. A bell rang in the distance as I spoke, sending an echo down my spine.

"Ah yes. I studied with the abbess long ago at my root temple." The holy man smiled at me from the core of his being and peace filled me within. I had done the right thing by the spirits and my ancestors. "Send her my regards," the abbot said. I nodded as a family came up to me, their eyes shining with tears and awe.

"Miss Kim." The father of the family, wearing a suit, nodded to me. "We are grateful to you. If you need anything while you are in Huế, please let us know. My sister is now safely with us."

A little girl in a pink dress, her hair tied in tight pigtails, emerged from behind him.

She raised her arms to me, and I picked her up with my gloved hands. Laughing, she turned to her family and beamed.

"You can help so many people," the abbot whispered to me. "You have helped so many people, even without Việt Kiều bribes. You have a good heart."

Tears came to my eyes. "Of good heart" was my middle name, the word from our ancestral poem. The rightness of what I was doing filled me, and I bowed humbly to the abbot.

"I know something you could do for me," I told the father of the family. "I need to return to the centre of Huế."

I balanced on the back of the father's moped. Behind us the mother, two more relatives and the little girl rode on the other moped. A sense of contentment rose in me. My headache had disappeared, and the weight and misery of my morning experiences dissipated. I would endure much for the sake of these families and the ghosts. They could not wander around the spirit world, hungry, without the offerings of their descendants.

I got off the moped a block away from the hotel. The father pressed into my hand a lucky envelope and I bowed to them as they rode away, slipping the envelope into the back of my jeans as I walked towards the hotel.

Outside the hotel I spotted our chauffeur leaning against the wall, talking to a cyclo driver.

Ignoring my rapidly beating heart, I walked up to them.

"Did you enjoy your walk?" the chauffeur asked me.

"Yes, I did."

"Have you eaten?"

"No."

"We will eat in the hotel at six," he told me, then turned to the cyclo driver. I glanced askance at him. The cyclo driver, though tattered in dirty singlet and shorts, had clean fingernails. He was not what he seemed to be.

Warily, I returned to my room and at six went up to the hotel restaurant. The chauffeur was waiting there.

"Bác Phuc is attending to some Party business," he told me.

I ate alone, self-consciously, among the few foreigners in the restaurant, and when I retired to my room and shut the door behind me, I felt a premature sense of relief. Maybe I had gotten away with it.

A bell rang in the hollow of my soul. Opening my eyes, I saw chi Thinh and Bà standing side by side. This seemed natural to me – there were different rules on the other shore.

- I have met your guardian ancestor, Thinh said. *She is luminous, as if warmed from the inside. You are well protected, at least on the other shore.*
- You have done well, Bà told me, and I could not help but smile.

I opened my eyes to the insistent ring of my alarm. Calmly, I switched it off, the now familiar taste of salt in my mouth. I took a shower, filled with the blessing of the goddess, confident of my role. I almost looked forward to the first psychic shock of the day. Dressed once again in my soiled clothing, I waited for the knock on the door.

Half past four and no one had summoned me. I opened my door and looked down the corridor. No one was there. Curious, I took my key and closed the door behind me.

Almost immediately, the driver opened Bác Phuc's door and came out. He looked at my soiled clothing and gloved hands.

"Get changed into clean clothes. We aren't going to the site today. And pack the rest of your things. We'll be leaving in ten minutes."

His tone brooked no questions. I retreated to my room to pack. Then Bác Phuc himself was knocking on my door. He was smiling.

"We are going to the Marble Mountains. An American military expedition is there looking for soldiers missing in action. They heard rumours of us and asked to see us."

Americans?

Our driver fetched our luggage and accompanied us to the foyer, where the hotel staff were still sleeping on mattresses on the floor.

"They may ask us to accompany them back to America with the remains we identify," Bác Phuc's eyes were alive in a way I had not seen before.

The driver unlocked the hotel door and led us out to where the car was waiting.

"Would you like to go to America, Kim?" Bác Phuc asked.

"Of course," I said, almost too quickly. I'd never been outside of Việt Nam.

"We'll go together," he said warmly as we got into the car. I smiled at him and his dark eyes wrinkled in appreciation.

"Get some sleep if you can," he told me as the car pulled away. "It's a few hours from here."

When I woke up, Bác Phuc was conversing with the driver. Then he turned to me and smiled again. The transformation in the man was incredible. But I could not smile after the first two days of working as a psychic.

"There was a US airstrip from China Beach to the Marble Mountains. And an infirmary hidden in the caves. There were many remains for their teams to work over. I wonder if they have psychics of their own," he mused.

"I know that their psychics have their own TV shows, but I've never heard of them working for the MIA teams," Bác Phuc continued.

"I don't know if their psychics are real," I boldly said. "What's on TV is different from what I experience when…"

Bác Phuc met my eye and nodded. For the first time I observed that he was handsome for an older man.

"We can find out later," he said, and then stared out the window.

I caught a glimpse of a giant white Buddha raised above the green paddy fields. "Made of marble?" I asked.

"Yes," Bác Phuc said, lost in thought.

I observed him out of the corner of my eye as we neared our destination. Bác Phuc had been kind to me in a distant way before today. I never forgot that he was my superior.

But today he told me what he was thinking, and he was excited about maybe going to the States. Just like I was. Maybe we were not that dissimilar, since we were both psychic...

"There are stories about Quan Âm performing miracles during the war in the infirmary at the base of the cave. You may like to visit it," he said. I smiled at him and when he smiled back I felt a jolt not dissimilar to the spark from the dead.

We arrived at the Marble Mountains. Their peaks reached for the sky, and the grey hewn rock reminded me of the islands of Ha Long Bay. There were stalls selling drinks and marble statue souvenirs at the car park, and I belatedly thought of shopping for my parents and sister.

The Americans arrived soon after, with a Việt Kiều interpreter, driver and guards. The American flag flew prominently from their sedan, and I wondered if this was wise.

"You must be Bác Phuc," the Việt Kiều interpreter said, rolling up his shirt sleeves in the heat, and it was obvious by his milky white skin that he had not seen much of the sun and by his towering height that he had never missed a meal in his life.

There were three white Americans – two men in army uniforms and one woman in a business suit with trousers. The Americans talked to the interpreter and among themselves.

"My name is Khôi," the interpreter said. "MIA retrieval is an ongoing concern to the American people. We hope you can help us identify the remains and graves we have found while being here."

"How are they going to recognise what we see?" Bác Phuc asked.

"I don't know," Khôi said. "But they know what battalions were stationed here."

"Then they'll know who is missing," Bác Phuc suggested.

The interpreter shrugged and turned to the woman who was talking to him.

"They would like to take you to where the airstrip was and then work from there."

We went back to the car and followed the lumbering sedan down a dirt road. "We know where the airstrip was but it's better to not let them know we know," Bác Phuc confided in me.

"Do many Americans come over to make peace with the dead?" I asked.

"Yes. They are haunted by ma hon, the hungry ghosts that died violently far from family and friends."

"Are you haunted by hungry ghosts?" I boldly asked. Bác Phuc closed his eyes for a moment. Then he opened his eyes, his gaze far away.

"I was haunted by my unit. Most of them died in an ambush. But I found them and put them at rest with their families. That's how I came to work for the government as a psychic."

The silence in the car was so still that it was unnerving. Then Bác Phuc seemed to return to the here-and-now.

"The work we do is important," he said again.

I bit my tongue, wondering about the Southern ghosts. It was wrong that we were pleasing the Americans and could not find peace among our countrymen, I thought.

We pulled up at the edge of a beach. Stepping out of the car and buffeted by the heat, I wanted nothing more than to go for a swim in the water. But instead we began to walk along the beach. We wandered further inland, past the salt brush and palm trees. Then the Americans stopped suddenly.

"This is where the mass grave is," the interpreter said, as one of the men paced around in a circle. I braced myself for the heaviness of the work and pulled up my shirt sleeves.

The Americans had spades and began to dig into the soil. Some locals came by to see what we were doing, and one offered to show the Americans more graves for a fee.

Bác Phuc took him aside, and the man disappeared into the brush as quickly as he appeared.

"These are my best friend's tags," Mitch, the largest of the white American veterans, said in mangled Vietnamese. I held out my hand for the twisted tabs of metal and jolted as they hit my skin.

"We're going on a no-fire mission. Just play this over the PA."

The dark cigar-like insides of a plane and four grunts of agreement from figures sitting wedged in beside each other.

Then the noise, a howling playing loud from the speakers on the plane. The words: "You will be haunted into the next life if you continue this war," in grammatically perfect Vietnamese, accompanied by the howling of the wind.

The hairs on the back of my neck stand up as the plane flies on. Then it is fired upon as it turns for the airstrip.

No wonder, I thought, shaking as I handed the dog tags back. The Americans had played on the Vietnamese fear of the spirits. They did not know that what they were messing around with was real. Looking at the wide eyes of the American before me, I realised that he now believed.

"I know what we did was wrong," he said hoarsely, tears in his eyes. "You are so gracious to help us." Mitch gave me a hug and I stiffened, not knowing what to do. Bác Phuc caught my eye and nodded. I hugged him back, as though I could forgive him, and let him go.

We continued our work, finding Southern Vietnamese as well as American remains.

I found myself daring to identify the Southerners in front of the Americans to see what Bác Phuc would do with them.

The Americans, solemn and serious, treated them as if they were their own. Khôi, the interpreter, raised his eyebrows occasionally to me as if I were doing something wonderful. Bác Phuc did not show any emotion at all. I began to wonder if he was just saving face.

When the sun had reached its zenith in the sky and they had called it a day, I looked at Bác Phuc again. He was exhausted, I sensed, but still maintained his bearing.

"We'll have lunch at the Marble Mountains and then we can visit the caves," he said.

The Americans joined us for lunch, sitting awkwardly on the platform under the tarpaulin that served as a cafe. I drank a can of Coke without stopping – I was that hot and thirsty.

"You have a rare talent," Khôi translated. "You must come and visit us in the States." Mitch smiled at his own words.

Khoi winked at me, and before I could stop myself, I smiled. I looked at Bác Phuc and he nodded.

I wondered at the bravado of Khôi. He appeared to be unaffected by what we were doing, and the Americans treated him as an equal. He looked young, and seemed to have taken a special interest in me.

After lunch we went as a group to walk in the limestone caves. They were refreshingly cool. I accidently brushed a hand against the walls of the cave and was assaulted with images.

Moaning and screaming in pain.

People dying in their own filth.

A rare occurrence, the saving of a life.

Weary nurses and doctors.

Shivering, I held my arms to my sides. Bác Phuc seemed unaffected as he walked on ahead. I found myself walking beside Khôi. He towered above me, and now he looked at me with wide, dark eyes.

"Were you born in America?" I asked him.

"Yes, I was. My parents were boat people."

I asked the question that was burning in my mind.

"Do they think that Northerners are still the enemy?"

Khôi thought for a moment before answering.

"My mother is wary of coming back. I have told them that the war is over, but for her the war is never over. She is happy, though, that I have a job that brings me back to my roots."

"How old are you?" I asked him.

"Seventeen. I'm in an accelerated course at college."

Seventeen? He was only a year older than me.

"You must come to the States. California has great beaches," he said, staring at me. Then he dropped back as the Americans gestured to him to take some photos.

We began to descend some stairs and I remembered the myth of Quan Âm at the base of these mountains. We reached the bottom of the cave and up ahead I saw a faint source of light, a hole through the roof. The sunlight slanted down to cast a halo of light around a small painted statue of Quan Âm.

Was that it? I swallowed my disappointment. The statue was only knee-high.

An old woman came up out of the gloom, carrying sticks of incense. Bác Phuc intercepted her and bought some. He gave half of them to me.

When I accepted the incense I felt a gentle jolt, and felt a sense of his good regard for me. I smiled and his eyes creased and smiled back. Feeling warm despite the coolness of the cave, I let the old lady light my incense and I bowed three times before Quan Âm.

May I be doing the right thing by the dead.

May my family and… Bác Phuc be happy and prosper.

On the way back to Huế I held the marble statues I had bought for my family on my lap. Bác Phuc had bought a jade pendant and slipped it into his pocket. I began to wonder whether he had a girlfriend in Hanoi. All of a sudden it mattered to me very much.

I slept a little and when I woke up I found him looking at me kindly.

"It's exhausting work, isn't it?" he said.

"Yes," I replied.

The car drove us to our Huế hotel. As we pulled into the car park, Bác Phuc reached into his pocket. He gave me the jade pendant.

"I noticed you didn't buy anything for yourself at the Marble Mountains," he said.

"Thank you. That's very nice of you," I stammered, feeling my face warm. I touched the cold stone with my fingers, feeling the exhaustion of the young boy who had polished the stone.

"You deserve it," he said.

That night, Bác Phuc accompanied me to dinner. He guided me with his hand on the small of my back and I felt the import of his touch. That evening he asked about my family and my sister's fiancé. I found myself telling him about my grandmother and how she always made offerings to the spirits. I kept the visitations of the Southern spirits to myself.

I did not notice that Bác Phuc had not told me anything about himself until I was in my room alone, reflecting on the day.

When I lay down to sleep, I wondered if the spirits would visit again. I found that I hoped they would.

This time the girl soldier had someone else standing beside her. It was a young Vietnamese man with white skin who towered above her and when he saw me he smiled like a bolt from the blue. It was Khôi, the interpreter.

I felt the surge of energy between us and was captivated by his large brown eyes and flawless white skin.

He smiled again and I could not help but smile back. This was like nothing I had experienced before.

- *He is like you,* the girl soldier added.
- *It is good to meet you*, I said, and this time the empty greeting had meaning for me.
- *Do the Americans doing MIA work know you are psychic?*

He smiled and gently laughed.

- *They do not believe in psychics in America the same way as in Việt Nam. The military cannot be seen to use psychics*

in America, even though they do in Việt Nam. I'm a college student, and I study parapsychology in theory, not in practice. But I dream of ma hon, the hungry ghosts. Many descendants are in America.
- *So you work for Việt Kiều*, I said.
-*Yes. In America it is better that people generally do not believe in psychics. It protects us from trivial pursuits and the attention of authorities.*

I nodded, even though the situation seemed totally foreign to me.

- *I was thinking we could work together, you in Việt Nam and me in America. Although, I have been told the situation is complicated here,* he continued.
- *Yes,* I confirmed. *Southern Vietnamese are not given the same respect as Northern Vietnamese or Americans. But in the eyes of Quan Âm there are no sides in conflict.*

Khôi seemed to understand instinctively what I meant.

- *So you would need to do this privately if you wished to.*
- *Yes. My boss is a psychic too. I don't know if I can hide it from him. Unless I give him a cut of my gifts…*

Khôi frowned.

- *If only your military was as forgiving as ours.*

It took me a moment to realise he was talking about Americans being more forgiving than the Vietnamese. This Việt Kiều was large for a Vietnamese and had probably been fed lots of cows' milk to make him that way.

- I will keep in touch with you, he said. If you don't mind.
- Yes, please. I tried not to sound too desperate.

He smiled at me again as he began to fade. The girl soldier waved at me happily before disappearing. Then I woke to semi-darkness as the sun rose behind the curtains in my room.

7

I arrived home, wondering what I would tell my parents. The jade pendant from Bác Phuc felt warm on my neck.

I was greeted by my sister as I came up the stairs.

"Would you like some pho?" she asked, warily.

I got up and went into the kitchen. The maid was busily preparing a bowl of pho for me, the way I liked it, with fresh chilli and pickled onions. Ma was sipping at her tea. The money was nowhere to be seen.

My sister finally said brightly, "At least you're here for my wedding. You can try on your áo dài."

I shivered at the thought of the burgundy áo dài that I had already worn in dreams.

"I need to have a nap," I mumbled. The toll of the last few days had caught up with me.

I ate the pho but did not taste it. Ma opened her present and stroked the white marble Buddha gently.

"That is a nice jade pendant you chose for yourself," my sister said, her present unopened.

"Bác Phuc bought it for me," I said. I heard Ma take in a breath. The air was weighted with meaning.

"Our relatives are coming over tonight," Ma said. "Do you want to invite Bác Phuc?"

I shook my head, my face reddening.

"I will see him in a few days," I stammered. I wasn't ready for the jokes and the scrutiny he and I would be subjected to, and retreated again to the room I shared with my sister, noticing now how cramped and cosy it was.

Opening up my handbag, I happened upon the red envelopes given to me by the grateful crowd the day before. They were thick with paper, and I assumed notes. Inside one lucky envelope were two hundred American dollars. I put it aside and opened another. It was a packet of folded white tissue paper.

Carefully, I opened it up on the platform that served as our bed. Was it jewellery? When I opened the last fold, it revealed shards of cleaned bone. I sighed. A folded piece of paper tumbled out of the little package. Opening it, I read the postal address of Chua Huong.

Maybe I can still finish my work, I thought. Sitting up straight, I braced myself and touched the shards.

In my mind came the silhouette of a male soldier walking up and down a narrow lane in front of a concrete shell of a house. He turned around, stood to attention and paraded down the lane as if unable to stop his patrol.

The war is over, I thought to him as I closed my eyes. The soldier in my mind did not respond, merely turning around and repeating his parade.

I withdrew my bare hand. Quickly, I turned over the piece of paper and jotted down what I saw. Then I wrapped the bones up in their package and put it back in the lucky envelope.

To my disappointment the other envelopes contained only money, which I collected into a wad, leaving aside 200,000 dong for myself. I was home.

I stopped by the post office that afternoon and sent the bones back to the temple in Chua Huong, before riding to my best friend's house, preparing a face-saving story for myself. Instinctively, I knew that I should keep my spiritual visitations to myself. I did not want to be exploited for my abilities and the past week had taught me that people only looked out for their own interests without consideration for my feelings, especially if they thought they could gain from my gifts.

"Kim!" Ngoc greeted me with a hug, the most enthusiastic welcome I had received since landing back in Hanoi.

"You would not believe what has happened!" She grinned and showed me her left hand. On her fourth finger was a ring with a glittery stone. I shrieked in girlish delight, truly happy for her.

"We have to get you a boyfriend," she schemed. "Maybe at your sister's wedding?"

I laughed. She was so self-absorbed that she had not noticed the new jade pendant that I wore. I forgot about my gift and my duties and immersed myself in gossip and wedding planning.

When I came home there were more parcels waiting for me. Intrigued, I opened them one at a time. The first contained the remains of a Northern soldier. The jolts and the death only made me flinch a little now. Bác Phuc was right, I was getting used to it.

Then I opened one that contained an ivory pendant of the Buddha. There was no message or return address. Was it a present? I touched it and was transfixed by the story that unfolded...

The sound of the bell returns me to my true home. Opening my eyes, I return from the depths of meditation, as if from underwater, from the ocean. The bell echoes in the hollow of my soul and beyond.

Breathing in, I am breathing in.

Breathing out, I am breathing out.

The sound of the bell penetrates my mind. Easing my posture I let go of my childhood memories, which float to the top of my thoughts like a leaf on a pond.

I am fresh, fresh as a flower.

I am still, still as a mountain.

Glass shatters and a ripple runs through the consciousness of the meditating monks and nuns. The hired mobs are back again. A rumour was whispered that the authorities in Bàt Nha paid villagers up to one hundred and fifty kilometres away to come and destroy the monastery.

I consciously breathe out my tension, trying to release my fear. In the middle of the sangha, circled by three hundred of my brothers and sisters, the practice is strong in the meditation hall. The terracotta Buddha statue at the front of the hall is still intact, though the white walls are filthy and desecrated with piss. In a brown nun's robe I feel visible, old and vulnerable, attempting to return to the island of peace and calm within, breathing in and out.

Na-mo Avo-li-ke-te-ra. Na-mo Avo-li-ke-te-ra.

We sing her name, Avoliketera, Quan Âm, the Goddess of Mercy, she who hears the cries of the world. In the courtyard of the temple there was once a white marble statue of her, holding a vase of water, her hand in a mudra. I dread to think what the mobs did to her.

I call her name. I do not know if she ever hears me.

The smell of incense infuses my robe and I return again to the peace within.

I feel the menace of the men surrounding us and feel sick in the stomach. We have gone without water and electricity and without much food for the past few months. Our practice has shone brighter as we starve and take comfort from each other's presence. But my fear nibbles at my peace, and I want to run again. Breathing in, I try to cradle my fear like a child, soothing myself. I feel vulnerable as a nun in a drab brown robe – the men are leering at all of us.

Sanctuaries are an illusion, only suffering is real. This is not what the Buddha taught, and my experiences forge my own sayings from his teachings. I believed that any safety I might find would only be temporary, any refuge impermanent. But my teacher would say, all things are impermanent and change. I hope that our situation will change. Some days I cannot not bear another moment of being under siege.

The rain falls in a steady drumming on the roof of the meditation hall. I catch myself swaying gently. Dizziness claims me for a moment, and I open my eyes. More men have come into the hall, this time carrying crowbars and hammers. Some have a different look to them, and a shudder runs down my spine as they methodically start banging at the meditation hall walls with their tools. Police, I suspect – they do not have the disorder and violent randomness of the other men. The Vietnamese, having no other enemy to turn on, are turning on themselves.

One of the men in particular has a military set to his gait and is directing others with hand signals, as if by not speaking he is keeping his distance.

Time is transparent to me, and I move in and out of my memories as my consciousness tries to resume its stillness.

Bad memories emerge and I try to not get caught up with them like the tide. To follow those thoughts would hook me back into the past. I sit and try to observe from a place of calm.

From my island inside myself I touch the roots of my suffering, live like a throbbing wound.

I retreat to the practice inside myself to release my anger and fear. Fear and anger are the enemy of mankind and the Communists are afraid of the Buddhists – President Diệm was afraid too once, so long ago.

Breathing in, I touch my fear.

Breathing out, I release my fear.

The PA messages are louder, stronger now, interrupting our meditation, denouncing Thich Nhat Hanh and ordering us to return home. The villagers, paid by the authorities to drive us out of our home, are harassing the younger nuns. My breath is ragged and I must calm myself, breathing in and out. I heard rumours that Việt Nam is now the chair of the Security Council of the UN. Two monastics from America came here and witnessed what was going on and then our water supply was destroyed. We hoped that the US embassy staff would come and visit and see for themselves the destruction of our home. The smell of smoke permeates the hall from the fires lit outside.

We were warned. Why? The question was asked, and word filtered among the monastics that the last time Thich Nhat

Hanh visited Việt Nam he asked for the religious police to be disbanded. He was too popular, a sister whispers. In the four years that Prajna was open to the public many thousands of young people came here, many to become monastics.

The seeds of violence have been watered in these people. I am frightened but I resist the urge to act from my fear. Fear and anger are the enemy, not mankind...

As the rain pours down, more men enter the meditation hall. The wind and rain blow in through the broken windows. We are ordered to stand up and move. There are many of them, three times as many as us. We are pushed and shoved. The most senior of us stands and nods for us to obey. Frightened, I follow my sisters as we are expelled into the pouring rain.

Outside, the destruction is apparent. Only the rain stopped the fires that burnt down the walls of the nunnery and Buddha Hall. The statues of a woman holding the hands of two children are now armless and the children beheaded. The Avoliketera Quan Âm statue has been reduced to a pile of rubble. Stumps and broken tree trunks litter the yard where we used to do walking meditation. The ground is now churned up by thousands of feet and the smell of petrol lingers in the air. We are herded out of the Prajna gates, leaving our home behind.

The mob have left us standing in the rain and are returning to the monastery with their hammers and axes to destroy what remains.

"Go to Phuoc Huế Temple in Bào Loc." The suggestion spreads and we begin to walk, then run, into the rain. Mud squelches between my toes and I become drenched as we hurry towards sanctuary, fifteen kilometres away. Behind us the security police have lined the road, urging us away from the monastery. I stumble on into the darkness, my hope destroyed.

Phuoc Huế Temple is small, a miniature set of rectangular buildings compared to the monastery we left behind. Its monastics hurriedly welcome us into their main hall. We sit together, jammed up, and the smells of sweat and damp penetrate our bodies.

Na-mo Avo-li-ke-te-ra. Na-mo Avo-li-ke-te-ra.

Someone whispers Avoliketera's name in a singsong chant and soon we all join in. Tears slide down my bewildered face. The last time we sang this joyfully we were clustered around the ornamental lake in Prajna. Today the chant is a cry for help and mercy. Outside we can hear the roar of police trucks and the growing sounds of the crowd.

We are blasted with orders over loudspeakers to leave the temple and return to our homes. But Prajna is my home.

The abbot was asked to expel us, but he refused. He was then threatened with the destruction of the temple.

Then a message comes from the Catholic Church. It has offered sanctuary if we are forced from the temple. Outside, one or two of us reach the internet and telephones to make our plight public. Small hope kindles in me at the tentative smiles of the younger monastics. Someone begins to sing about the island home inside the self.

I want to return to my island...

Then one of the older monastics ventures in from the outside, bearing food from concerned villagers in Bào Loc. And a message from Thich Nhat Hanh himself.

"Prajna is now legend. You carry the seeds of Prajna inside you to spread to the world."

Blinking back more tears, I recollect the running of the waterfall down my spine and the calm of the white, seated Buddha statue that used to watch us walk beside the creek. Unbidden, the white serene face of the statue of Quan Âm's smile surfaces once more in my consciousness before disappearing.

I prayed to the goddess outside of myself for so long. Now, with my home destroyed and the police baying outside for us to leave, I must find sanctuary inside myself again.

The small hands of my sisters find mine in the siege and instead of despair at their grasping I discover the strength in their practice. With the strength of the sangha I retreat within myself and meditate once more. The sense of "no-self" and the interconnectedness of all things emerges from me again.

We inter-be and inter-are. Even if we were sundered, a part of us will always be at Prajna. The monastery might be destroyed but we will always carry the seeds of insight inside us. I remember this as the final deadline is read out. By New Year's Eve we will have to leave the temple and surrender to the police.

So we disappear. I hug my sisters one by one, offering them comfort. Like little brown sparrows, we disappear one by one into the night. I bow to the senior monastics one last time, a profound stillness settling over us all. I remove my monastic's robe and surrender it to them, to shuffle off into darkness.

I let go of the ivory Buddha and sat back in shock. This was not history. This happened late last year, and the man with the military gait had a familiar stance to him. With a chill I realised that it had been Bác Phúc directing the destruction of the monastery.

Why? It made no sense. Buddhists were pacifists and apolitical. And the nun was so young…

And why was this sent to me? Was it a warning? I stared at the benign face of the Buddha pendant. What was I supposed to do?

I decided to go to the temple for advice again. I parked my moped and looked quickly around. No one was following me. I calmed myself – the pendant's visions were making me paranoid.

I was greeted by a novice who asked me to wait for the abbess. I sat on a stone bench, hearing the murmuring of mantras in the background. It soothed my fears, if only for a little while. The abbess came out, pacing slowly and deliberately, immediately calming my racing heart.

"Daughter, what is troubling you?" she asked.

We sat down on the bench together and I produced the white Buddha from my handbag.

"This was sent to me without a return address," I began. "It shows a monastery being destroyed by the police in Bàt Nha…"

The abbess took in a breath and the expression in her eyes sharpened. Instinct warned me to be quiet.

"Officially," the abbess said, "Bàt Nha monastery was destroyed by a rival group of Buddhists."

My eyes widened. This was so obviously a lie that the government *must* be hiding something.

"The monastics have sought refuge in Thailand," she continued. "They are following Thich Nhat Hanh." This agreed with my vision. It must be true, then, though I really had no doubts. I just didn't want to think…

I kept silent about Bác Phuc's actions in the destruction of the monastery. He was a dangerous man. I had known this, but his kindness had made me wonder… What was I going to do?

"You must do what Quan Âm would do. If you follow the eightfold noble path, you will find an answer," the abbess said. I realised that I had voiced my last thought aloud.

"No harm. Relieve suffering," I said.

"Yes. You have been given a great gift. You will see truths that other people cannot and gain wisdom."

Tears were threatening to break me down in front of the abbess. She understood in a different way from how Bác Phuc understood.

"Is there anything I can do for the temple?" I asked, and realised I was asking both for Prajna monastery in Bàt Nha and the temple I attended.

"Spread the word as far as you can," the abbess said. "Knowledge is power. We do not want to overthrow the government, but the truth must be known." I nodded grimly. Maybe I, too, would have to go into hiding. I left the temple planning what to do with my new knowledge.

That night, Ma and Father regaled the guests about how fortunate they were that I was home for the wedding preparations. No mention was made of my gifts, or that I wore gloves throughout dinner.

I overheard one of my more distant relatives ask Father how I was doing. "She works for the government," he said, and no more questions were asked that night. Maybe Father was showing caution at last, I thought, and then, more cynically, I thought that perhaps he wanted to keep his good luck to himself.

Sure enough, past midnight, as the guests thinned and it was only my family left at the table, Father turned to me, drunk, and ordered me to tell my sister's fortune.

"We need to know if this match is a lucky one. You can tell the truth to your immediate family…"

"It *is* lucky," my sister protested. "The astrologer said so."

Father belched and gestured at me. "Take your gloves off."

Reluctantly, I obeyed. My sister offered her hands to me, and I clasped them. There was no jolt this time, just a gentle blending. Closing my eyes, I saw my sister being comforted by her husband. She was crying.

Why did she leave me? Instinctively, I knew she was talking about me. I let her hands go and opened my eyes. My family leant into me eagerly.

"Your husband will be good and comfort you," I said in a monotone. A headache was building up behind my eyes. I had drunk little that night and was bone-tired. Wreathed by my family's smiles, I made my excuses and went to bed.

The night passed without dreams and when I woke up the next morning I felt strangely bereft. After all the psychic work I had done and the contact of the spirits, home was mundane, grey and lifeless. My sister snored gently next to me, her body casually close to mine again. I would not leave this place. Would I? All I had done was to support my family.

It was a week until my sister's wedding. All the guests were making their way to Hanoi. Our cousins from far-flung places, even one who was studying in America, had come back to celebrate. Groaning at the thought of more relatives, I fell into uneasy slumber.

The next day Khôi turned up on our doorstep. He asked me out for coffee and I agreed, to the delight of my parents and sister.

"Do you know of any Việt Kiều psychics?" I asked him once we had settled at a café.

Khôi's face fell.

"They're mostly older people who are scarred by the war. You are the first one I've met that is my age. Once they knew I was going back to Việt Nam they stopped talking to me."

I raised my eyebrows.

"Việt Kiều politics can be complex too. They will call anyone a Communist for daring to have anything to do with Việt Nam. Even going here on holiday. If you use the Southern flag in an artwork, they will accuse you of dishonouring the flag, no matter what your intentions are," Khôi told me.

I shrugged in response. In Việt Nam people used the image of Ho Chi Minh on watches and clocks. But you had to get a permit to stage an art show. I began to see the intelligence of Khôi hiding behind the bravado. I found I liked this man better.

"Are you going to be a leader like your mother?"

"No. I just want to play guitar. But I don't think I'll be able to."

Silence fell as he drank his coffee. "We have five days till we leave. Why don't we go to Sapa? I've heard its gorgeous…"

"I haven't been there," I mumbled.

"Come on, it will get you away from the spies outside your house. And you have to go. Everyone has heard of Sapa."

It was true. I had heard of the ethnic minorities and the beauty of the mountains.

I agreed to go. Then Khôi kissed me on the cheek goodbye, and I began to look forward to it.

That night, the other shore was crowded with grateful spirits. They reached for me with silvery hands and when I reached back they piled on top of each other in an effort to touch me. Thinh, Bà and Khôi were nowhere to be seen.

I tried to call out to them, but I was muffled in the grey twilight.

I was hiding from the French.

I was being chased by Bác Phuc.

My monastery was being destroyed.

My skin burned in fire…

I was all the ghosts and spirits. The pain in the ground bore me up and I opened my mouth to scream…

8

It was five o'clock in the morning and I was myself again. My body was rocking to and fro and I recognised we were in the sleeper carriage of a train. Underneath me in the bottom bunk bed, Khôi snored. Next to his head was an empty tin of beer.

So that was why he was not on the other shore. He was drunk.

My parents had agreed, almost eagerly, when Khôi asked for their permission to go to Sapa with me as his local tour guide. My Northern accent would enable us to get local prices for everything. If Khôi had gone by himself he would have been charged three times as much, with his milky white skin and expensive clothes. While I was out of the room they must have negotiated a price. When I returned Father was pocketing American dollars.

"Negotiate well for the Việt Kiều," Father had whispered as he said goodbye.

I stared at the ceiling of the carriage, overwhelmed by what I had experienced. I wanted to wake Khôi up and ask him if he had ever experienced such things. Instead, I glanced out the narrow carriage window as the sun rose, spilling pink light onto the glass. I tried to empty my mind, but memories kept flickering like flames at the edge of my consciousness. Everything I had tried to forget was coming back to haunt me.

I murmured the Heart Sutra under my breath as the train rolled into the station. Quan Âm could listen to all the cries of the world. I needed her help to survive what I had learnt in the past week. All the history of Việt Nam seemed to weigh on my shoulders.

Khôi staggered up and banged his head against my bunk. "Sorry, Chị Kim," he murmured, then fetched down our luggage from the overhead shelving. We stumbled outside onto the platform and went out onto the street to a café where the buses to the mountains waited.

Through some canny negotiation I got us onto the first bus. And then I saw two men muscle in on the queue, shifting two local Vietnamese tourists out of the way.

"Hey, we're being followed," Khôi sounded excited, almost delighted, and I could have hit him. Of course Bác Phuc would protect his investment.

The two security agents shoved themselves on the bus a couple of seats away from us. I ignored them and tried not to slap Khôi, who was exclaiming over everything in this rural precinct.

The bus clambered slowly up the mountains. I became pre-occupied with my thoughts. I did not want to talk to Khôi with the security agents within earshot. He happily bought overpriced snacks for us to eat and seemed so jovial compared to when we had been in the Marble Mountains that I was reluctant to burst his bubble and get his serious self to speak to me.

But even I was distracted when the bus turned a curve and the layers of the Sapa mountains came into view. The rice terraces were a rich green and the grey mountains were shrouded in mist. The Marble Mountains were dwarfed in comparison to this.

Khôi was trying to take pictures with his mobile phone as the fog lifted into the sky with the sun's rays. For a moment I was glad I came. Then my gaze happened on the security agents. One stared back at me dispassionately. I was nothing to them, I realised, just a job.

I clasped my gloved hands together to still their shaking. Anything could happen to us out here and no one would know.

We booked into the most popular hotel, with a view of the mountains. We had separate rooms, for which I was grateful. I did not feel the urge to know what happens after a man's kiss anymore. Khôi barely noticed the bedroom set-up, and was more concerned with venturing out to explore as soon as he put his bags away.

"We have to stay where there are other tourists," I told him. His face fell, but my point was made when we went up to reception and the security agents were sitting on the couch opposite the front doors of the hotel.

"We can go on a tour of the plateaus," I said to Khôi. He brightened at that, and I negotiated an inflated price with the hotel staff, checking my messages and e-mails while we waited for the guide. There was nothing from my sister or my parents, nor from my best friend. Suddenly I felt cut off from everyone I knew. I hoped nothing had happened to them… Even if Bác Phuc knew I had helped out the Southern ghosts he wouldn't punish my family without arresting me first…

When the tour guide arrived, he found he had an extra two people in his tour. The security agent spoke to him, and the face of the tribesman darkened. We were joined by a white couple and three backpackers. For once I was grateful for the presence of foreigners.

As we exited the hotel we were swooped on by young girls in indigo skirts and leggings trying to sell us jewellery. One grabbed my arm. I shook her off just as I got a flash of the poverty her family was in. They could only afford new clothes once a year, at New Year, when they carried apricot tree branches to market to sell to Hanoians.

I closed my eyes momentarily. I could not give to all these people. I was emotionally drained enough from the Southern spirits.

I joined the others walking down the concrete road that wound down the mountains. The two agents looked bored as I maintained my silence, while Khôi made friends with the white English couple and chatted to the tour guide.

The tour guide's English was impeccable, with traces of an American accent. Every now and again he glanced furtively at the agents, but their presence did not stop him explaining the history of the Hmong people in Sapa.

We descended off the main road to walk towards the rice plateaus. The mist had almost completely gone, and the sun shone brightly on the mountains, though our breath still steamed when we talked. I wondered whether what we were hearing from the tour guide was being altered to suit the agents from Hanoi. Khôi seemed oblivious and questioned the guide about the conditions that the Hmong lived in.

I marvelled at the heights of the mountains and their grey beauty. I felt swallowed up in the landscape as we headed down into the green valley. It made me feel insignificant, my concerns dwarfed by the immensity of the landscape. I was glad.

We reached a cluster of shanty-like houses and were greeted by more Hmong girls bearing jewellery and purple-dyed throws. They also showed us outfits like the ones they wore themselves: indigo skirts with colourful belts and headbands.

One of the girls suddenly seized my hand. I had foolishly left my gloves at the hotel. I received flashes of working in the fields, and the ease of hawking in comparison. Then I saw how she was beaten if she did not make enough money. Tears came to my eyes and the young girl stopped tugging at me and peered at me instead. She asked the tour guide if I was all right.

The world reeled around me. I was drowning under the weight of the visitations I had had. Khôi was standing over me, asking what was wrong. Then I blacked out.

You are Kim Nguyen. You are not the real Kim Nguyen, but you are descended from her to help the world.

- Bà?
- Miss Kim?

I was engulfed in flames. My flesh burned and I could not retain my pose. Again, I was shot and buried alive in a mass grave. I struggled to breathe but could not. I was drowning. But this time no one saved me, and I swallowed water when I tried to call out.

Kim!

It was Khôi, holding my hand, and I got the sense that he drank to cope with the visitations. Then I was flooded with his regard and concern for me. It was too much. I took my hand away.

When I came to, I found myself siting on the concrete floor of the shanty, Khôi by my side. I could see the other tourists gathered outside, along with the security agents.

"Are you okay?" Khôi asked me.

"It's too much. It's too much," I babbled. When I closed my eyes, I saw the Americans in a fighter plane waiting to attack. The National Liberation Front being bombed with Agent Orange. Pain and suffering in the hospital in the Marble Mountains.

"Kim?"

I saw refugees huddled in fishing boats sneaking past Communist guards. I saw torture at the re-education camps. The pain and suffering seeping through the ground capsized my consciousness. The wars fought by the Hmong people for independence.

"Stop," I whispered. "Stop it. *Stop it!*" I buried my head in my hands, pulling at my hair to stop the images in my head.

The tour guide came in, concerned.

"What is wrong with her?"

One of the security agents followed him in and walked up to me, pushing Khôi aside. I begged him not to touch me, but he held me by the upper arm for a moment and it was enough for me to see that he was one of the tails assigned to Bác Phuc. He was ex-military and viewed following us as an easy job compared to killing foreigners. I did not want to know how he killed them, but the details came regardless of my protests. He had raped and murdered Southern soldiers, and villagers who had hidden insurgents.

Terrified, I flinched away from him and held my hands out for Khôi – amazingly, he managed to get on the other side of me and clasp my fingers. I felt, once more, Khôi's fondness and respect for me. I saw the large house where he lived with two brothers, a mother whose years of hardship showed in her eyes and a kindly father with bad memories.

"She needs to rest. We'll go to the hotel," Khôi told the guide.

"Those security agents are following us. They can escort us back," I found myself saying, before my common sense could tell me otherwise.

"I know," said the guide. "The local shaman is my mother. She may be able to help you."

Were there psychics everywhere? Now I could sense them, they were so common that it was amazing the government had not recruited more of them.

"Thank you, but I think it's better if she gets bed rest," Khôi said. The guide looked at him for a long moment then said nothing.

Shaman. The culture of ethnic minorities like the Hmong was on display at the Ethnography Museum. It was official policy to not discriminate against them. But I did not want to see a Hmong shaman.

"Can you get up, Kim?"

I struggled to my feet. The white couple came in, and the older man introduced himself as a doctor.

"If there is anything I can do…" he said in fluent Vietnamese. The guide, Khôi and I were shocked to silence. "I think if the young lady believes she is a psychic and is overwhelmed by visions she may be suffering from a disease of the mind."

I waited for Khôi to speak but he did not.

"I'm not sick in the head," I said, and found myself looking at a patronising gaze that I knew would only see illness when I spoke.

"I can recommend some good doctors in Hanoi. You should return there straight away," he told Khôi. I belatedly remembered that Khôi was hiding his psychic ability. The deception had trapped me, though, in the care of this doctor.

Khôi thanked him and typed the doctor's referrals into his phone. Once we had left the tour party the two security agents followed us as we walked up the path.

I felt swallowed up by everyone's concerns. When I closed my eyes I saw flashes of orange, of fire. What was happening to me? It was like I was having a breakdown of the mind. Suddenly I was scared. Just suppose Khôi took me to a hospital? Or to a shaman? Neither appealed.

The security agents did not help. One was talking on his mobile phone.

When we reached the hotel, Khôi escorted me to my room. Under the watchful eye of the hotel staff he could not come in – it would be improper.

"Call me if you need anything. Just rest now," he said. I shut the door on him and lay down on the double bed. My eyes closed and I descended into chaos.

I was being raped by American soldiers.

My body turned to ash in the fire and a gag was being forced into my mouth.

I killed children. They were spies for the Viet Minh.

Blood was on my hands, sticky and gory.

I called out to Bà to help me.

Suddenly I was back on the other shore. I felt Bà's hand on my shoulder.

- *Quan Âm hears the cries of all humankind. She is a bodhisattiva. While you are still a child.*

I began to cry. I wanted to be an ordinary teenager now. I didn't want the psychic gift anymore.

- *If you seriously wish for that, take the Western medications,* Bà told me.
- *Would they make my gift disappear? Would I still be able to see you?*

Bà smiled sadly.

- *No. I and Thinh are your spirit guardians. We can stand by you while you suffer through these visions. Just call to us and we will come.*
- *I didn't kill children, did I?*
- *No, you did not.*

I closed my eyes. When I opened them, I saw Khôi standing next to Bà.

- I'm sorry, Kim. I could not out myself as a psychic to those people. How are you feeling?

That a boy would ask me how I felt was beyond me. My regard for Khôi grew stronger. I understood then how my sister must have felt for Hieu.

- I'm feeling weak and I have a headache, I told him.
- I have aspirin if you want it. Are you still seeing visions?
- I did.
- There is a train back to Hanoi tonight. Shall we catch it?
- Yes.

I could not keep the relief out of my tone.

On the train ride, we had the carriage to ourselves.

"How do you manage all the people's stories?" I asked Khôi.

"You know how I cope," Khôi said, gesturing to the beer bottle in his hand. "But seriously," he continued, "I was taught to ground myself before each seeing and to come back to myself afterwards. So I have this token that I hold." He showed me a jade Buddha on a cord around his neck.

Here was someone who understood. I felt myself softening towards Khôi, despite his drinking.

"Do you have a girlfriend in the States?" I asked, bracing myself for the answer.

"I did. We broke up the week I left for Việt Nam. She didn't understand me or my gift."

We got to Hanoi at five am and shared a taxi – back home for me and to the hotel for Khôi.

"How much longer are you going to be here?" I asked him, wondering if I could invite him to my sister's wedding.

"The MIA team is here for another week. I haven't decided whether I'll stay on," he told me, honestly. "Come visit me in the States." Then he kissed me on the cheek goodbye.

9

At home again, I unpacked and thought about where I could get a spiritual token like Khôi's. Then I remembered the jewellery that I had been given when Bà had died. Rummaging under the bed, I found a box wrapped innocuously in plastic bags. This would be it.

I uncovered the wooden box and opened it. I could not help but be distracted by the other objects in the jewellery box – the little gold anklet I had been given when I was one month old, a pair of jade earrings that had been Bà's favourites. Then I found what I was searching for. A miniature jade pendant of Quan Âm on a gold chain. Touching it, I felt the warmth of Bà's skin and the peace in her nature after the wars. I could wear this and maybe it might help me summon Bà as well. I put it on next to the jade pendant Bác Phuc had given me. I wondered momentarily why I had not seen Bác Phuc on the other shore. Maybe his gift was different to mine and Khoi's.

I felt lucky to be the girl I was. Khôi thought I was special, I suspected, and so did Bác Phuc. Khôi drank too much but Bác Phuc was older and more serious. I did not know how to choose between the two of them. I smiled to myself in anticipation of what might unfold.

The next day, I was sipping coffee from a glass when Bác Phuc came up the stairs with Father trailing behind him.

"Your services are required again," Bác Phuc said, smiling.

Startled, I got up from the table. I put on my gloves and followed him to his moped.

Bác Phuc drove speedily away from my home and turned down the main street. I expected to be taken to the barracks, but instead we pulled up three blocks short.

"Come in for some coffee," Bác Phuc invited me. We walked through a laneway to a house with a padlocked gate, and the hair on the back of my neck prickled as I went through the front door. I turned around to find Bác Phuc locking the gate behind me.

I sensed the house was empty as I walked into a living area with cream couches and a glass coffee table. Taking off my shoes, I sat down at his instruction.

"Wait here," he said, disappearing into what I presumed was the kitchen. Then he returned with an envelope. It was the envelope containing the ivory Buddha that had betrayed the destruction of the temple. He casually placed it down on the coffee table between us and folded his arms.

"Kim. You know that we are constantly monitored. What possessed you to do this? Even after I warned you."

His statements, once oblique, suddenly crystallised in my mind. Bác Phuc was a psychic too. Suddenly frightened, I felt as if I was naked under his eyes. I crossed my legs and swallowed.

"I do what the goddess tells me to do," I said bravely. I had done nothing wrong.

"You are a government employee, Kim. Quan Âm is a superstition."

I blinked at him, appalled at his blasphemy.

"Parapsychology is a science. Spirits and ghosts are real, but loyalty to the old gods and goddesses is only for the masses. Not for people like us." He shifted in his seat, his eyes hard, and continued patiently, as if to a young child. "As your mentor I am also your monitor, as was the driver in Huế. You have slipped up. You know you are not supposed to support or aid those who are against the government. It's lucky I caught you just in time. We knew you had gone to Chua Huong temple, against instruction, without me or your driver. We waited until there was evidence to convict you. There is enough here to court martial you as a traitor to the state. But I believe in your naivety."

I stared at him. A benign, almost fatherly expression came over him, and I clenched my gloved fists. I was too scared to think of something to blank my mind. I could only think of my family.

"Kim, your talents are too valuable to be wasted in a re-education camp. I will protect you – this once." He smiled at me, and a chill ran down my spine.

"What will you do?" I asked, trying not to shake.

"I will protect you. But in return you will marry me."

My mouth fell open.

"You are a kind, sweet, young girl. You will make a good wife. Don't worry, we will wait till after your sister's wedding before announcing it. Then she won't get jealous." His intricate knowledge of my family dynamics rendered me helpless.

"I'll return you to your family now. Would you like to see the house you will live in first?"

I was still shaking when I arrived home. Bác Phuc let me get off his bike and make my way up the stairs unhindered, unlike when I was in his house, trapped and alone.

Feeling filthier than I ever had when I was in Huế, I took a shower. I imagined the imprint of his hands still on my body. What was I going to do?

I changed into a plain T-shirt and tracksuit pants. I wanted to hide and disappear. This was what I had foreseen. I wanted to run away.

I took off the jade pendant he had given me.

Where could I run to? I could not tell my family of my foolish actions and my shame. I had endangered them all.

I put on another pair of gloves and prepared to ride my moped to the temple. The abbess was a friend, and I had to deliver the greetings of the abbot from Chua Huong to her. Then I checked myself. Would they follow me there?

Would it be a betrayal? Would the abbot of Chua Huong be placed under house arrest?

I cursed myself and my gift then. Too much responsibility made my head hurt. Surely the abbess would have advice for me. It would not be out of character for me to go to the temple, I reasoned. If they followed me, I could say I was visiting to honour my grandmother's memory.

Going out of the house, I looked to my right and left. A cyclo driver lounged in front of our house, dirty and tanned bark-brown. Ordinary people walked by, shoppers and high school girls giggling on mobile phones.

Taking a deep breath, I straddled my moped and cautiously pulled out into the road. No one followed me.

Parking in front of the temple gate, the sound of the monks chanting reached me. As I stepped into the temple courtyard the stillness of the place caught my breath and my mind slowed down. Frangipani petals lay on the concrete, and I picked up a fallen blossom as I stepped carefully towards the meditation hall. The spoiled white petals reminded me of myself, the slightly rotting scent a sign of my new life.

A novice in grey robes, walking slowly, met my eye and bowed to me. I bowed and asked to see the abbess. She bid me wait in the courtyard, so I sat under a tree as the monks chanted on.

Form is emptiness, emptiness is form...

The chanting was of the Heart Sutra. What was I going to do?

It seemed like forever until the abbess came out, her gentle smile lifting my heart.

"Daughter," she greeted me, and tears came to my eyes at her kind face. "What has happened to you?"

Sensing a sympathetic ear, I told her of the deceased in Huế, my breaking of the rules in identifying the Southern folk, and when I reached Bác Phuc's threat I came to a shuddering stop. I could not tell her what had happened to me. I was too ashamed.

The abbess bowed her head and took a deep breath.

"This man is not a good Buddhist, nor a good Vietnamese," the abbess said. "Does your family know?"

"No. They could do things to my family, send them to a re-education camp…"

The abbess nodded, her eyes full.

"Sister," she said, gifting me with kindness, "It must rest heavily on you, having to reunite so many from the other shore to their descendants." I burst into tears again. Truly, the abbess understood. "You are not the only true psychic – some have hidden their talents among frippery to avoid the attention of the psychic bureau. The work is being done, quietly, even here."

My gaze deepened into hers and suddenly I wanted to take off my gloves and grip the abbess' hands to confirm my intuition. She was smiling at me, and I realised I did not have to confirm what I knew to be true.

"Oh! I send you greetings from the abbot at Chua Huong," I told her belatedly. Her smile grew deeper, and she nodded. "Could I become a nun like you?" Nothing seemed more attractive to me then in that moment. I did not want to be a woman anymore.

"It will not protect you from Communist interests," the abbess said. "Somehow you must find a way to make them lose interest in you."

"Bác Phuc wants me because of my psychic ability," I said, and then an idea came. Jumping up, I thanked the abbess profusely and ran to my moped. I headed towards Ngoc's house. The abbess' parting words warmed me.

You are a daughter of compassion. Of good heart. Even my grandmother's photograph seemed to embrace me from the ancestors' shrine.

A sudden honking shocked me out of my thoughts. I slammed on the brakes of my moped just in time to avoid hitting a bicycle. Behind me the honks continued as I instinctively put my foot on the accelerator, sweat running down my brow. My mind was clear now, for the first time since returning from Huế.

I thanked Quan Âm for sparing me yet again from a tragedy as I pulled up onto the pavement in front of my best friend's block of flats. It was here I could put my plan into action.

I walked up to the front door. No one seemed to have followed me, but I took no chances. I would do what they would expect me to do. See my friends and family.

I did not have to hide my nervous shaking as I greeted her. She immediately asked me what was wrong.

"I just had a moped accident. I fell off the moped. But I'm all right now," I said in response to her fussing. She put her arms around me comfortingly. I received flashes of her boyfriend and, distracted, I shook her off. "I'll be fine."

She sat me down and we had some tea. Then I craftily executed my plan.

"I've been selfish lately. You asked me for a psychic reading, and I didn't do one for you."

Her eyes lit up and my cynicism rose as she held out her hands for me to hold.

I stripped off my gloves and held her hands. Unsurprisingly, her thoughts were full of weddings and what to wear and whether it would be fashionable or not. *Once, my thoughts would have been like this*, I despaired.

"I can't see anything," I lied. I frowned and let go of her hands.

"Maybe you are still shaken up by your accident," she suggested.

"Maybe. I'll try later."

"Tuan is talking about me to all his friends. That's got to be a good sign. What are you wearing to your sister's wedding? It's so generous of you to give her your pay… What was Huế like?"

I laughed, trying to recapture what remained of my girlhood. "Boring. Backward." I found myself unable to tell her of what I had experienced. I didn't want to ruin her optimism with what I had learnt about men's nature. Instead I lost myself in a flurry of gossip about my sister's upcoming nuptials.

A few hours later I again took her hands in mine. Tuan loomed large in her mind, his caresses and kisses. Immediately I felt nauseated and told her I could not tell her fortune anymore.

"Maybe," she said brightly, "your accident took your gift away the same way it came."

"What am I going to tell Bác Phuc?"

"You could pretend," she suggested. "Most psychics are frauds anyway." The thought made me smile genuinely for the first time since returning from Huế.

I retreated to my room to count my money. The money that was promised to me for going to Huế had yet to appear. I would have to give most of it to my parents. But after that… there may be enough for me to go to America.

I decided to use my psychic gifts to flush out who I could bribe. Bác Phuc couldn't touch me once I was out of the country.

My thoughts strayed to the American psychic, Khôi. He wouldn't want to touch me once he knew what I had been through… and he would know as soon as he saw me.

Besides, I wouldn't want him to get involved with the security police in Việt Nam.

Tears welled up inside me and I choked them down, not wanting Ma to hear me cry. I curled up under the quilt on our platform bed and closed my eyes.

- *Miss Kim? Miss Kim!* I opened my eyes to see my soldier guide to the spirit world.
- *I'm pretending I have lost my psychic ability to get away from Bác Phuc*, I said.
- *Who is Bác Phuc?*

Surprised, I told the ghost what had happened to me. Finally I was able to cry noiselessly in the silence.

- *He's dangerous,* the ghost said. *I'd shoot him.*

I stifled a laugh.

- *Where am I going to get a gun from?*

The spirit looked at me and, sobered, I remembered that she had probably shot people during the war.

- *I will tell you if I see him,* the spirit reassured me. *Rest now.*

When I woke up I stumbled down the stairs to see my parents. Only Ma was home, preparing for the wedding. When she saw me, she smiled at me benevolently. Her gaze moved to my collarbone, where the jade Quan Âm pendant nestled.

"You found Bà's necklace," she commented as I sat down opposite her. "That was her favourite necklace." She paused, searching my face as though she could read my secrets. "Bà was right. I never say so in front of your father, but she knew about the ancestors and the spirits and how important they are. Sometimes she would use a Ouija board to try and predict the course of the wars. I would stay up at night and spy on her. She predicted the North would win the war. You are her granddaughter."

Her words felt like a blessing to me. Even Ma now understood, even though Father did not. She looked at me again.

"She is with you, isn't she?"

"Yes," I replied. Ma smiled and held my hands.

"Daughter, is she well? Does she like our offerings?"

"Yes." I felt the pull of how important it was for Ma to know, and I knew I could not continue the charade of losing my ability with her just yet.

"I wanted to protect you from the past. You're so young. But the government have other plans for you," she continued.

I swallowed. I wanted to protect Ma from everything that had happened to me. I wanted to lean my head on her shoulder and cry.

"Have some tea, daughter," she said, and I let the moment pass by.

The morning of my sister's wedding came. She did not sleep well, and I was kept awake with my scheming thoughts. She was nervous when I helped her put on the traditional red áo dài.

"This does not bother you?" she asked as I brushed her hair in preparation for her trip to the beauty salon.

"I've lost my psychic ability." I told her of the accident, trying to ignore her tension for the ceremony ahead. She was too preoccupied to sympathise.

After she left, I put on my burgundy áo dài. I wished suddenly that it was true, that I had no ability, and I could be as shallow as my best friend and think only of my family and my wedding. The weight of what I was hiding burdened me.

I told my parents of my lost psychic ability over breakfast and their faces fell.

"You have to inform Bác Phuc," Ma said.

Even the mention of his name made me sick to the stomach. He was the one person who could catch me out, and he was coming to the wedding reception. He would want to feel… I pushed the thoughts away. I'd be with the bridal party. The groomsmen would be my companions and he wouldn't dare try anything in public.

It began with the tea ceremony at our house in the morning. My sister and Ma were radiant, Father solemn as the groom asked them formally to take my sister away to his house. As they declared their acceptance, sudden tears came to my eyes.

No one was truly going to marry me. I wished I could see into my own future in America. I did not want to leave my family, but I had no choice. They would thank me when they came to America. Tears fell on my silk áo dài and a dark splash widened like a blooming flower.

At the groom's house a roast pig was served for lunch and my sister was given a ruby necklace and bracelet. Her eyes shone and Ngoc, holding my hand, was envious.

"My fiancé had better take note of this," she muttered in my ear.

I was listening to the recital of our ancestral names. My name, Nguyen Kim, and my poetic lineage name, "of good heart." My grandmother would approve of this marriage.

So did the multitude of far-flung cousins and relatives who awaited the reception.

Finally, the reception – the event I had been dreading. I kept an eye out for Bác Phuc among the guests. I helped my sister with the white train of the Western wedding dress she had changed into.

At the bridal table, the first course arrived, and he did not. I sipped at the champagne and the fizzy sourness took the edge off my anxiety.

Bác Phuc did not appear until the sixth course. He saw me and inclined his head.

I went through the motions of the toasting and accompanied my sister, holding her train. I smiled at the cameras, my jaw hurting and my stomach cramping. Finally we reached Bác Phuc's table.

The bride and groom received showers of congratulations. Bác Phuc's eyes were on me and I felt naked under his gaze. But he did not move from his seat and we left the table.

The bridal waltz began and the hair on the back of my neck prickled. I danced the first dance with the groom's brother, who complimented me on my beauty, but by then I was too tired from tension to smile.

My gloves protected me from the battering of psychic flashes as the second dance began. In the bare, off-the-shoulder Western-style dress I wore I now felt like I was half-naked.

To my relief, he released me. I returned to the bridal table, wanting to throw up.

I sipped more champagne till my cheeks were rosy with alcohol. Then Bác Phuc approached the table.

"May I have this dance?" He was distant like he had been on the last day in Huế. My parents, a table away, were watching what I would do. Reluctantly, I took his hand and let him lead me onto the dance floor.

"You don't need your gloves anymore when you are with me," he whispered into my ear. His breath stank of alcohol and his sweaty hands slipped onto my waist. "Take your gloves off," he commanded, and I obeyed as the dance ended. He clasped my hand in his.

I was flooded by frustrated desire counteracted by heavy disappointment. *Useless female*, he was thinking. *How am I going to get promoted now?*

I had to will my face to be still as the realisation hit me. Bác Phuc was a fake! He could not continue to be promoted without a genuine psychic by his side.

"I'm disappointed in you," he said, his words echoing his thoughts. "The Bureau will not require your services anymore. I have given your parents the remainder of what you earned in Huế. They will take good care of you."

He let go of my hand and I almost sank to the floor in relief, then he turned his back and strode off out of the restaurant. I stumbled to the bridal table and sat down.

Then I smiled.

I could hardly wait to see my sister and her husband off to bed. Now that Bác Phuc had left, I naively believed that I was free of his attention. So I joined Ngoc and Tuan at a late-night karaoke bar once the formal reception was over.

I returned to my normal self that night, once again just another sixteen-year-old girl. My life as a psychic seemed to be a fading nightmare under the glare of the disco lights and the throb of the beat from the cheesy American rock songs we sang.

I noticed that my psychic power seemed to be dampened by the alcohol I had consumed, and I could not sense anything about my best friend as she wished me good night.

I came home, head reeling, to an empty bed and collapsed there, still dressed.

- *Miss Kim, Miss Kim.*

The soldier girl was in her best dress, a simple white tunic with trousers. Her eyes shone, freed from the pain of being a hungry ghost. In her arms were flowers, offered by her descendants.

I strove to get away from her. I didn't want to be psychic anymore. But instead she came closer to me, her skin luminous in the twilight of the spirit world.

- *You are in danger, Miss Kim.* She voiced the words and I thought I could read her lips as they moved.
- *From what?*
- *The Communists have real psychics among them. They will soon know of your plan.*
- *Go away!*

I made the warding sign against spirits to her, and she flinched. But as she faded away, she mouthed another warning.

- *Be careful, Miss Kim. You are of good heart...*

10

I woke up, the sun of the morning pouring into my room. The bed was empty without my sister and my head throbbed. I winced against the light and got up to pull the shutters closed. I could barely think through my headache as I somehow changed into jeans and stumbled down to the kitchen.

Ma and Father were already awake. They were counting the lucky money they had received from our guests. The maid took one look at me and served me coffee. Ma smiled at me and I grimaced back.

"I'm glad you are home," Ma said. "Don't worry about the government job. You can still read people's fortunes here."

"I can't read people's fortunes..." I protested weakly, as I sipped the too-strong coffee.

"It doesn't matter," Father cut in. "You cannot let me down now. You can pretend – you are a smart girl. Our friends and their business friends are counting on you."

"But that would be..."

"Just tell people what they want to hear," Father ordered, and I knew from his tone he would not brook argument.

I sulked into my coffee and breakfast pho. I wanted to rest. I needed to sleep. I wanted to run to the temple and ask the abbess to tell me my fortune.

"I'm going to the temple today to bless my sister's marriage," I said.

Father looked at his watch. "This evening you are to be here for my business group," he said. "You will teach their sons and daughters English."

I nodded valiantly. The words to thank him stuck in my throat. Suddenly I thought it would be no loss to be far away from Father. This heretical thought dizzied me. I could be a psychic in America, like the spirit mediums on their TV programmes. Theirs was a free democracy. But Ma...

Before I left for the temple, I kissed her on the cheek. She batted me away, but I could tell that she was pleased.

Getting on my moped, I noticed the same cyclo driver sleeping in his cab opposite our house. I sped off and took a different route to the temple. Hunched over the handlebars, I was beginning to see the same people around me. I knew almost everyone within a block of my house, I told myself. Of course everyone seemed familiar...

This time I arrived at the temple with flowers for my grandmother and a donation for the temple. I parked my moped and as I walked into the courtyard the abbess greeted me, frowning.

"The police were here earlier," she said to me.

Ashamed, I fell into step with her as she walked around the courtyard.

"I'm sorry. I brought this upon you. I should not have come here."

The abbess shook her head.

"They have checked on us before. This time they asked about you, whether you were gifted or not and whether you had performed any rituals here. I told them you were an ordinary girl."

I smiled. It was the first time I was glad to hear I was just an ordinary girl.

"The spirits told me –" I started, and the abbess put her finger to her lips.

"We have a sister temple in Orange County. I taught one of the senior nuns there. Bác Diệm. Perhaps you can send my greetings to her."

Silenced, I looked into her chocolate-brown eyes. Compassion lay there, and sorrow.

"This is not a good place for you anymore," the abbess said. The dismissal cut me to the bone. I wanted to cry again but willed myself to stillness.

The abbess gently touched my arm and turned to the shrine we had walked to. Quan Âm rose above the shrine, her benign gaze looking down upon me.

"She is always with you, little Kim." In the distance I heard a bell chime. It echoed in the base of my spine. "Wherever you go, remember her and her blessing."

My tears had been replaced by an eerie calm. The abbess produced a crumpled piece of paper from inside her robe.

"This family owns a travel agency. They can get you an ordinary travel visa without questions."

Tears sprung to my eyes again, this time from gratitude. Swallowing, I bent my head close to hers and whispered to her about Bác Phuc's fraudulence. She listened and nodded without smiling.

"That such a man can be in such a position tells me he is dangerous even without a gift," she said to me.

We sat on a bench listening to the rise and fall of the morning mantras from inside the meditation hall.

Form is emptiness, emptiness is form.

I remembered the heightened sensations I had felt when I was first gifted, with the words of the Heart Sutra. Reciting the Heart Sutra mantra, I thought about the cresting wave of my sister's desire, the warm taste of beef soup and the soft smell of frangipani. I remembered how happy I had been when I could reunite the spirits with their descendants. After my encounter with Bác Phuc the last thing I wanted was to be touched by a man. Even a gentle man like Khôi was repellent to me.

"Maybe I'll become a nun in America," I said after a while.

The abbess held out her hands to me for the first time and I clasped them.

A sense of clamping down around my skull. Darkness. Then a still room. An all-seeing camera, an electronic eye in the corner. A window with bars…

I took in a breath, and the vision stopped as I met her concerned expression.

"Daughter. Sometimes what I see does not come true. These are possibilities, no more. You must be careful."

Terrified, I nodded. Sound came to me again, the twittering of sparrows and the chanting of Quan Âm's name.

"There is someone I want you to meet. If you go to America maybe she can accompany you. She is an American citizen." The abbess left me sitting on the bench.

I swallowed and looked at the sparrows in the courtyard, so free. The abbess returned with a novice. Her head was shaven, but her eyes shone like the abbess' eyes – she looked like someone who had found peace and joy in the world.

I stood up and bowed to her, and she bowed in return.

"Hello, sister," she said, and the voice sounded familiar. I knew what the abbess was going to say before she said it.

"Tam is from Prajna monastery. As you know, most of the monastics fled to Thailand. But she wishes to go back to the States."

"The world needs to know what happened at Prajna," the novice said.

"The family travel agency should be able to organise tickets and visas for you both. They may want a gift in return, though," the abbess said.

I left the temple with her blessing and more than I wanted to know.

That evening I braced myself for another onslaught from Father's friends. After the terrors of the war in Huế I did not fear what possible secrets these men could have.

I recognised some of the food as leftovers from the wedding banquet, but said nothing.

Father did not drink and neither did his business associates, who instead contented themselves with tea and congratulations to the father of the new bride.

Some of them I hardly knew and one I did not recognise at all, which made me instantly suspicious. When it came time for me to hold their hands, I had already concocted a lie for him.

His hands were clammy, and his closed posture showed his boredom with the company and bragging of the other men. But when he looked at me with heightened interest, he instantly reminded me of Bác Phuc. He was military, I guessed, and I touched his hands reluctantly.

Swallowing, I reared away instinctively from the confirmation of my thoughts about his nature. Planted among boring international businessmen, his true purpose was to monitor international trade and movements of Việt Kiều businesses. Only the flimsiest pretext saw him in this pathetic middle-class dining room with this child playing at len dong.

"You have romance coming into your life," I intoned, trying not to show my nervousness at his disdain.

"Sure, I always do!" he said. Only his mouth smiled. Instinctively I let go of his hands and turned to the man beside him. I faked the next reading too, and the next, until I saw the first man's attention turn back to Father smoking cigars.

The conversation turned to local politics and I cringed for Father, willing him not to speak his mind in front of this security agent. But he did.

"Bloody Central Bureau. They hire my daughter for only a week then let her go." To my shame, Father's indignation was genuine, but I felt a flicker of affection towards him. *He does care about me*, I thought, staring at my now-gloved hands.

"You just need a good husband," one of them joked to me, as if he had not said it a thousand times already. I pleaded a headache and retreated into my lonely room. Looking around the walls and hearing the men downstairs, I suddenly felt trapped.

Outside my window the cyclo driver was eating some noodles and chatting to the noodle vendor. I imagined, as they glanced up, that they could see me through the leaves of the shutter. Sitting down on the bed, I put my head in my hands and despaired. Wanting only to escape, I changed into my pyjamas, even though it was only eight o'clock, lay down and closed my eyes.

This time Thinh was accompanied by Khôi and when our eyes met, I felt an echo of the jolt I had felt before. Was this what falling in love was like? I only had more of my sister's memories to compare it to.

- *You must escape*, said Thinh without preamble.
- *They will learn of you, and they will hunt you down. Bác Phuc destroyed the home of the monastics, and he will destroy your home.*
- *How do you know about Prajna monastery?*
- *There are psychics in the monasteries, as you know.*
- *Come to America*, Khôi said. *I can protect you from the authorities here.*
- *I don't want to leave my family.*
- *They can come later.*
- *Are there only three of us?* I asked Thinh.
- *There are others in America, and other parts of the world.*
- *What about the other psychics in Việt Nam?*
- *They have their own spirits to look after. You found me, so I am with you.*
- *Did you know Bác Phuc was a fake?*

*- I wondered why I had never seen him. We are merely
immortal, not omniscient.*

Chided, I stopped questioning her.

*- I can't leave the country without them knowing,
I despaired.*
- You can use your gift to find out who to bribe, suggested
Khôi. *I bet you could get out without a record showing.
I did it in America, at LAX.*
- Why did you need to do that?
- I wanted to test my abilities, Khôi said, in all seriousness.

I did not understand. If I was caught, I would be put in
prison or under house arrest.

- You would be able to do it too, Khôi continued.

I began to feel afraid at what I might have to do and the
consequences if I got caught. In America, it seemed, things
were very different.

- We'll leave for the States together.

Hesitantly, I told him about the novice, Tam, and the
abbess' request.

- We will manage, Khôi said, with his customary bravado.
*I did not know that the government was still oppressing the
Buddhists.*

I was silent in the face of his naivety, which I once would
have shared.

I woke up with salt in my mouth and a stomach ache from tension. Somehow, I had to break the news to my parents that I was going to America.

And I may not be able to come back, I thought. I wanted to cry again at the injustice of it all. I did not know much about ordinary Americans. They lived in large houses and were concerned about love, mostly, or so I thought from their television shows.

11

I concocted a plausible tale before I went down to see my parents. Father and Ma were eating breakfast. Ma was weary from all the celebrations, but she managed a warm smile for me. Father just grunted.

"I've been called by Khôi, the Việt Kiều interpreter. He has asked me to go to America with him for a few weeks to do some work there." I hoped the truth that I had stretched did not show on my face.

"America!" Ma was delighted. "Does he know you have lost your psychic powers?"

"No, but I can fake it," I said. "They will pay me well."

Father was enthusiastic. "You see. You can manage anything, my clever girl." Once, his praise would have made me happy. Now it made me sad.

"When will you go?" Ma asked.

"In a few days."

"They want you that much?" Father commented. I was so relieved by their response and barely managed to stomach my breakfast.

Ma asked me about Khôi and I told her what I knew but did not reveal his psychic ability.

"He must be a genius to be in college already," Father said.

I wondered whether Bác Phuc had approached my parents for my hand in marriage and my stomach clenched again, making me want to throw up. I left my parents smiling and retreated to my room.

I felt trapped.

To my surprise, Khôi sent me a text that evening saying he would come the following day. I felt more relaxed from his words, and was able to think clearly about my sister and her husband. They had already left for their honeymoon.

I tried called my sister but was met by her voicemail greeting, so I texted her instead. I looked around my lonely room and it only now seemed to sink in that I was leaving my home. Outside, the cyclo driver still sat and I dreaded every visitor who came into the shop, thinking each was going to be Bác Phuc.

I decided to wait till Khôi arrived before buying plane tickets for Tam, the novice, and myself. Somehow I thought that if there were an American as a witness they wouldn't apprehend me in a public place.

I spent the day packing. When I lay down to sleep, I wondered who would visit me.

Instead I found myself on the other shore. Across the river were my parents, my sister and my best friend. Bà was by my side, a comforting presence.

But then I found myself drowning, and this time in the luminous grey light there was no boat woman to save me. I was being pushed down under the water and when I looked up I saw it was Bác Phuc in a boat, his face murderous.

I woke up with a scream on my lips. What was that dream? Was it a warning? Had Bác Phuc traversed the river between life and the other shore?

I walked down the stairs on slippered feet to the ancestral shrine. Bà smiled at me from her photo, and I took some incense, lit it and offered the sticks to her memory. It was four in the morning, and I did not sleep again.

When Khôi arrived, he was greeted by my parents. The sound of American-accented Vietnamese came up the stairs and I hastened down after running my fingers quickly through my hair.

"Kim, it is good to see you!" He smiled warmly at me, and I could not help but smile back at him. Out of the corner of my eye I saw my parents exchange approving glances.

Suddenly I was fed up with their matchmaking. There were more important things for me to do in life than get married.

"Shall we book some tickets?" he said, then turned to my parents. "We will have coffee afterwards, so we may be a few hours," he told them. Ma and Father nodded at his deference and wished us farewell.

"There is a government agent outside," I told him once we were out of earshot from my parents.

"The cyclo driver," Khôi said immediately. "I hired a moped. I doubt they will do anything while I'm around, being an American government official and all."

As we drove to the travel agent, I asked him something I had been wondering about for a while.

"How did you get your government posting?"

"My mother is a Việt Kiều community leader. The Americans asked her for someone to interpret and she volunteered me."

"Oh," I said. I looked behind us and did not sense anyone following. I relaxed as we pulled into the travel agency. "Let me do the talking," I told him. They would charge a Việt Kiều double for a plane ticket.

Buying the tickets was easy once I had mentioned the abbess in passing. The agent did want a gift, as she had said, which I would have found extravagant once, but after the pay for my psychic work it seemed a reasonable amount.

Then we went for coffee. Our conversation was light in the presence of others, about Khôi's study, my schooling, music and films.

"Hey, why don't you come out to a bar with me tonight? Just to listen to some music. We're leaving tomorrow, after all," Khôi suggested.

"I…" I wanted to say no, I wanted to pack. But I saw the plea in his eyes, and I agreed to go.

The cyclo driver was still at his post when we came back. I began to wonder what his instructions were. Merely to report on visitors to the house? They had already sent another psychic in to check on me.

Then I wondered whether Bác Phuc was subject to the same scrutiny. Maybe that was why he had not appeared at my house yet. Feeling superstitious, I made another offering to Bà at the shrine. When I came into the kitchen, I saw that Ma was sitting with a cup of tea. She spotted me and beckoned me to her.

"You have become more filial of late, daughter," she said to me. I sat down opposite her, thinking of my impending departure.

"I loved Bà too. I knew she was right to honour ancestors even during doi moi when we had to hide our offerings. I never said this to your father."

I nodded, now fully understanding why.

Ma sighed. "We've all been affected by the war," she said. "I sometimes have nightmares about it. But I didn't want you to be affected by the war."

I burst into tears at her kindness. I had hidden so much from her in order to protect her, and she in turn had hidden her experiences from me.

Ma held my hands and all I saw was her love for me, from when I was a little baby and continuing until now that I was a young woman. I sniffled back my tears and gave my her a kiss on the cheek. Then I retreated to my room like the coward I was, unable to say goodbye a final time.

I was still working out the implications of leaving for America when Khôi came to pick me up. His face was slightly flushed, and I knew he had already started drinking.

"Take your passport just in case they want identification," he told me.

I picked it up and inadvertently picked up the plane tickets as well. I stowed them safely in my handbag and went down to say farewell to my parents. They nodded at me and Khôi and we left together.

The cyclo driver appeared asleep in his cab as I hopped on the back of Khôi's moped. Then we went to the top jazz bar in town. I ordered a fruit cocktail while Khôi ordered more beer. He was tired and going from what I'd seen of my Father's behaviour when he drank I guessed that Khôi might become weepy soon.

"I love Việt Nam," he confided in me. "But I am treated as a stranger here, in a way that I'm not at home."

"Will I be safe in California?" I asked him.

"Yes, you will be. Once people know you've defected, they will understand. My mother will find you a place to stay and you can choose to go to school, or work privately as a psychic. Or maybe do both. You'll have to learn English, though, if you go outside the Vietnamese community."

"I can understand the meanings behind people's language but not speak it myself." I described to him the meanings I had picked up from the white Americans he worked for.

He grew thoughtful and mused: "Maybe that's why I find speaking both languages so easy. Almost simultaneous."

The jazz music seemed to hypnotise Khôi and he did not even drink from his beer when the solo saxophone was playing. I found myself appreciating the music too.

When we got on the moped to go home, I thanked him for the evening out.

"Not a problem. I'll take you to some good music in Orange County. You'll love it."

We were pulling up close to my house when I recognised a moped parked in front of it.

I pulled on Khôi's arm. "Don't stop. Keep going."

He did not ask me why until we were a few blocks away.

"Bác Phuc is at my house. I don't want to see him. He… hurt me when we came back from the Marble Mountains."

"What did he do?" Khôi asked. I fell silent, unable to describe what had happened to me.

"Bastard," Khôi said. "Have you told the police?"

I was shocked into silence. "He is a Communist agent. He *is* the police." I told him.

"Shit." Khôi turned left.

"Where are we going?"

"Back to my hotel room. I'll sleep on the couch – you can have the bed and tomorrow we'll leave for America. I'll contact the embassy and let them know we are leaving."

Tears of gratitude sprung to my eyes. I thanked the goddess I had the plane tickets with me. "But what about my parents?" I asked forlornly.

"You can ring them from America. Hey, they won't do anything to them, will they?"

My mind had started working again. "I can blackmail Bác Phuc. He is a fake psychic."

"Really? He could have fooled me," he said.

"The abbess at the monastery knows too."

"Cool," he said as he pulled into the Hilton car park.

While he called the embassy, I sat on the couch and fretted. Finally, I found the hotel stationery and wrote a letter disclosing Bác Phuc's fraudulence. I addressed it to Bác Phuc himself.

My mind whirled with the possibilities of what could happen until I fell asleep on the couch, fully dressed. Khôi was still on the phone, arguing in English.

The next morning, Khôi had ordered room service and I choked down croissants with my coffee.

"We have to fetch the novice from the monastery," I said. "She's a US citizen."

"I have some bad news. The embassy has only promised consulate assistance if we get arrested. That's all," Khôi said, his fist clenching and unclenching.

"If we can post this letter it may help," I said.

"I'll get it couriered," Khôi said grimly.

I wondered at the Việt Kiều's naivety, then remembered that a month ago I would have been the same.

We caught a taxi to the monastery, and the novice was waiting in the courtyard with a brown shoulder bag.

"The abbess was talking to the police," she said, and I saw the fear in her eyes.

On the way to the airport I kept waiting for us to be pulled over. The traffic flowed by, indifferent to our passing. Mopeds, cars, bicycles weighted with pigs and chickens sped past us.

This might be the last time I see my hometown, I realised, and a pit opened in my stomach.

What would we do if we were arrested?

My mind recoiled. All they had to do was put Bác Phuc near me and I would surrender.

We pulled up to the airport without incident and I gave Tam her plane ticket and passport. We were divided almost immediately at immigration, me in the line for Vietnamese nationals and the other two for foreign aliens.

My mouth dry, I handed my passport over to the uniformed official at the computer, sliding an envelope of money towards him.

"Miss Nguyen, proceed." He stamped my passport and let me through without using the computer reader that would have revealed all. As I went forwards to join Khôi and Tam, I glanced over my shoulder and saw the official on the phone.

My heart almost stopped. Tam came to my side and held me by the arm to guide me to our departure gate. We were two hours early.

"Relax, we're almost there. And we're flying on an American airline. There would be a fuss if they took either of you now." I didn't know about that, but I was happy for Khôi to buy us some more breakfast and coffee.

"How are you?" I asked Tam.

The novice looked at me. "I am okay, thanks. I am grateful that the two of you are coming with me. I fear for the abbess and what they might do to her. House arrest, probably. For hiding dissidents."

I swallowed. "I fear for my parents and the abbess."

We had an hour to go when I spotted a man in military uniform making his way towards our gate. My heart sank and the fear must have shown in my eyes.

"That's Bác Phuc," Khôi said, standing up.

"Sit down!" I hissed.

"He knows you are here." Khôi was right. Bác Phuc made his way unerringly to us. He was flanked by two other agents – the psychic who had visited our house and the official who had screened me in the barracks on my first day.

"Chi Kim. There's no need to be afraid. But we cannot let someone with your talents leave the country," Bác Phuc said.

"I wish to leave, and I have claimed asylum with the Americans."

"Really? I'd be surprised if they cared," Bác Phuc said dismissively.

"Did you get my letter?" I demanded. I saw his eyes shift and knew I had scored. "Let me go. Leave my parents and the abbess alone and I will leave you alone," I said.

"We can't let you do that. Come with us and we will leave your parents and the abbess alone."

Part of me wanted to yield then, and I almost believed him. But I saw the tension in the other two officials, and I knew it was a lie.

"Bác Phuc, I will warn you one last time. If you don't let me go, I will have to reveal our secret. Not to the Americans but to your comrades. I think *they* would care."

Bác Phuc laughed. "What are you talking about?"

At that moment a large white American in an armed forces uniform shouldered his way into the conversation. I recognised him as the one I had comforted at the Marble Mountains, Mitch.

"What's the trouble, Khôi? I got your message," Mitch said.

Bác Phuc gestured at the two officials, and they retreated.

"You will never be able to return, Kim," he said with a shrug of his shoulders, before turning to follow his comrades as they left us.

"Don't worry about them, little lady," the American said. But I knew it was my threat that had sent Bác Phuc packing. Mitch had simply provided a face-saving excuse for him to withdraw.

His last words were a death knell in my heart.

You will never be able to return.

12

On my first day in Orange County, Khôi showed me to his place, a small one-bedroom flat with a shared kitchen and lounge room area. The furnishings were spartan, but I was comforted by the number of books and the laptop lying on the couch. I remembered that Khôi studied at college.

He then opened a window to puff on a rolled-up cigarette. At least, I thought it was a cigarette, until the grassy scent of burning herbs reached me.

I pulled my high heels off, walked over to him and handed him a lucky envelope.

"No," he said. "You're like family."

"Take it," I begged him.

He sucked in his cheeks and drummed his restless fingers on the windowsill.

"I can pay rent to you. Or I can find my own flat like yours…" I offered.

"No. I'd like you to stay with me. It's safer that way. I'll sleep on the couch until you find your feet. Stay here for now. If you are a real psychic, you'll be able to make money here. But you need to be discreet for the moment. Word will get around." Khôi raised his eyebrows to himself, as if he could not believe it. "I don't have money for a maid, so you'll have to clean up and cook for yourself, you know," he said.

I nodded eagerly. In return for staying here I would happily clean and cook for Khôi too.

He continued drum his fingers, thinking.

"Kim… I…" He got to his feet to stub out his cigarette. I glanced at him expectantly. "I hope you like it here," he said quickly, before leaving the room.

We went to the Vietnamese quarter in Orange County for dinner. To my overwhelmed senses it was like being in Saigon, except the air was clean and didn't smell of garbage. There were fewer people, and among the Vietnamese there were white Americans, some fat and flabby, and African people.

"Don't stare!" hissed Khôi to me, pinching my arm. No one here was wearing gloves and I wondered how I was going to cope.

Khôi bought me dinner – roast duck and roast pork with rice. I was shocked at the amount of meat heaped on the plate. After dinner we went to the supermarket and again I was surprised by the abundance of packaged foods. To my disgust, he bought frozen meat.

"I don't have time to shop every day. You can if you wish, but you need American dollars first."

Lying in Khôi's bed while Khôi lay on the couch in the living room, I felt tired, so tired I could not sleep. Instead I stared at the cracked white paint on the ceiling. The bed was uncomfortable, too soft with a mattress that sagged in the middle. The world see-sawed around me, and it hit home that I might never see my parents or my sister again.

I gulped back noisy tears, not wanting to disturb Khôi.

What have I done?

The next day I asked Khôi to go to the temple to see how Tam was settling in. I noted the small family altar discreetly tucked away in the kitchen at Khôi's apartment. Two sets of grandparents were captured in black and white next to the customary large red candles. The fruit at the altar looked fresh. Now I knew better than to take an apple and eat it. It comforted me that despite his worldly and beer-drinking ways, Khôi still honoured the spirits. Vietnamese used to call Việt Kiều mac goc – people without roots. I was still learning the truth of it, I thought to myself, as Khôi showed me out the door.

We got on a bus, and I stared out at the big blocks of land and houses going by. The kerbsides were lined with grass and trees and the sun was so bright I had to wear sunglasses. The bus climbed up a small hill and when it reached the top we hopped off near the temple.

When I saw the giant white marble statue of Quan Âm, I want to break down and cry in relief at the familiar sight of her calm face and flowing robes. Immediately I felt at home.

Khôi took me by the arm and guided me into the pagoda-style meditation hall. Vietnamese people milled about, pausing only at the sound of the bell.

The bell rang into my consciousness and something in me became settled for the first time since I'd arrived in America. Up the front of the hall was the familiar sight of the gold Buddha meditating. The sangha sat in front of the Buddha on their knees and the service was in Vietnamese.

"I'd like to see the abbess," I told Khôi.

"As you wish," Khôi said, looking at me strangely. I imagined for a moment that he had read my intentions, and knew exactly what I was about to do. Then I shook off the thought. That was impossible. I was still wearing gloves and a long-sleeved shirt.

The abbess was inside the meditation hall, leading the morning meditation. The murmur of the Heart Sutra reached me, and I wanted to sink on the floor in prayer with them.

Tam was up the front kneeling with the novices. When she saw me her smile pierced my being. She was so happy in America and the fear that had characterised her before had been sloughed off like old dry skin.

When the abbess emerged, I began to tremble like a new leaf.

"Sister," I bowed to her deeply. "I bring greetings from the abbess at Green Willow in Hanoi."

"She is just new," Khôi cut in. "This is Kim Nguyen."

"I am a psychic and I wish to serve the temple," I told her.

The abbess stared at me for what felt like a full minute, then looked at Khôi.

"Come this way," she said gently, and took me outside. Khôi followed.

"You really wish to join the monastery?" the abbess asked.

"Yes, I do."

"You will need to study first, and serve the temple as a lay-woman. But for now, join us for the midday meal and meet some of the others here."

I felt Khôi's eyes on me.

"It is what I truly desire," I said to her.

Khôi raised his eyebrows and I sensed him withdrawing from me. My first instinct was right. Khôi wanted me to be his girlfriend. Suddenly I wished I could withdraw my words. I didn't know what a worldly Việt Kiều would do with a Hanoi-bound girl like me. But even thinking of kissing him made me feel ill, so in my doubt and confusion I said nothing.

That night I texted my sister. She did not reply till the following day and only to ask for *Paris by Night* merchandise. She seemed to have bought my act of only being in America temporarily and I felt a twinge of guilt, which didn't go away even afterwards as I e-mailed my parents. Certain that I was being monitored, I kept my e-mail sparse and trivial. I wrote about the weather and the abundance of rich, fatty foods. Ma's reply inquired about my health and about Khôi. Father did not reply at all.

Through Khôi I met other Vietnamese students. Some of them were local Americans, their families from the South. I was first asked to use my psychic ability for a mother with cancer.

Sitting under the watchful eye of the goddess, I touched the older woman's hands. Even here, Quan Âm's compassion spread through my eyes.

I was overwhelmed by the older woman's pain. She felt helpless, just like when she had been on the boat coming to Malaysia, imprisoned below, stinking of piss and shit. She still hated the sight of the beach and couldn't understand why her daughter would go there for fun. Her suffering overshadowed the nervousness I felt for my own fate.

I came here by plane, by bribery.

This woman had suffered, like the people of the North. We all had suffered because of the war. North and South.

Closing my eyes, I searched for some hope to give her. To my sorrow, there was none. She would soon go to the mercy of the other shore.

"Your pain will be relieved in the near future," I said to her gently, hating the power of my gift.

Her eyes still lit up at my kind words and she thanks me profusely. We got up together to light incense sticks for Quan Âm.

I bowed my head and wondered why the Vietnamese here flew the Southern imperialistic puppet flag of yellow with three red stripes. They had oppressed the Buddhists and were corrupt. Khôi even knew of people in America who had protested against President Diệm. The answer came to me: it was a symbol of hope. Hope for democracy one day against the Communists. Democracy like what they had in America.

13

I joined the afternoon meditation and the familiar silence settled over me. Next to me Khôi was impatient but followed my actions regardless. My gift unravelled in the stillness, and I remembered the last time I had meditated freely in Hanoi. Touching the earth and chanting the familiar verses, I had come far, but I did not feel I had come that far at all.

I felt kinship with the Việt Kiều in exile. *I'm a Việt Kiều now*, I thought to myself, and sadness welled up in me. *But the breathing in and out of freedom, not having to look over my shoulder, is worth it*, I told myself.

There were Northern and Southern Vietnamese people at the temple mingling together. There was suffering here, like there had been suffering in Việt Nam. But here I could be free. I could practise my gift without censure and serve the spirits without fear of the government.

All these refugees, these Việt Kiều, seemed happy and well fed. There were no mopeds but plenty of cars, and Khôi told me they were just like the young people in Hanoi, with the latest phones and fashion trends. The older people had lines in their faces that betrayed their memories of war and deprivation, but even here they seemed to have reason to smile.

To my surprise I was able to tell everything to Khôi. Somehow, he had developed a world-weary presence and didn't think that I had made a mistake by not looking for a husband. He didn't want to marry until he had established his career, and he was uncertain himself whether he would return to Việt Nam.

Khôi was so kind to me. He treated me with respect and even though I was sharing his flat he hadn't made a move on me. Sometimes I caught myself wondering if I was disappointed that he had not.

Being near the university meant there were cafés and bookshops close by, though not with the same density or friendliness of the markets at home. I would try out my English whenever I went to cafés by myself and I marvelled at the Americans, who seemed to always be either overly bold or distant, depending on their mood. I missed Hoàn Kiếm Lake and the warmth of Hanoi. When it was cold, I felt at my loneliest – I slowly came to realise that I could not rely on Khôi for everything. I met his drinking buddies, but the bar they hung out at was as far away as Father's bia hoi by distance. In America women drank with men and weren't necessarily companions for the night.

I finally met his mother when she came one day to visit, bringing food for him. Khôi warned me not to let her know that we were sharing the flat, or that I saw him on the other shore.

"She is old-fashioned and will think you are trying to take advantage of me. My mother has pushed every ability I have. I'm in this accelerated course with twenty-year-olds because she wants me to be the best. I'm tired of trying to be the best. I just want to be a kid."

Suddenly I felt for Khôi, who had to hide his gift.

"How come you don't do readings for money?" I asked him directly, as we ate the microwaved pork with lemongrass that she had prepared for him.

Khôi looked away before answering slowly, as if he was picking his words carefully.

"People take advantage of you if you proclaim you have a gift. There is too much pressure to say only what they want to hear."

As he swigged from a beer bottle, I wanted to hug him for his insight. Maybe Khôi could really understand me, unlike Bác Phuc. Khôi was a cute American boy. I wondered why he was still single.

"Does the MIA team usually use psychics?" I asked

Khôi shook his head. "It's better for you that they do not. I don't know what Mitch will tell his superior. He's talked a lot about you."

I fell silent. My future was a blank slate now I was in America.

"Should I go to high school?"

Khôi chewed his lip before answering. "I would try a community college. You are sixteen, but you would have seen more of life than some of the people here who are over sixty. At community college you could study ESL and you can do an accelerated course like the one I do. Wait till the start of next semester and give it a go then."

I breathed out a sigh of relief. All I knew of American high schools from TV was filled with lipstick and boys' fascination with girls and vice versa. And that world seemed too far away and trivial to me now. I did not think I could pretend like I had in Hanoi that I was just an ordinary girl.

"Kim, I need to tell you something," Khôi said. "There is a network of genuine psychics that is mostly made up of Buddhists. I scout for them. So when I heard of you in Huế, I told them about you. I was instructed to help you out and to get you out of Việt Nam if it came to that. I'm sorry I haven't been open with you. But I was under strict instructions. You could only be told about us after you were away from Bác Phuc."

I pressed my lips together and stilled the urge to throw something at him. I was totally dependent on his goodwill and he had hidden this from me…

"Is there anything else you've hidden from me, Khôi?"

"I'm not going to hurt you or let harm come to you, Kim. I promise." I glared at him and said nothing. "I'm sorry I hid it from you," Khôi repeated and my anger turned into ash. It was the first time someone had apologised to me twice, and the first time someone had acknowledged I was hurt.

I nodded, wanting to cry at his kindness.

"You are safer staying with me until you are known and vouched for, Kim. There are Southern veterans here that survived the Northern re-education camps. They are unable to be fair to those who speak with a Northern accent. They view me and mother as traitors."

I shook my head, astounded. Khôi was so young, like me. How could they think that we were like Bác Phuc?

Mitch invited both Khôi and I over for dinner. When we arrived together at a brick house in the suburbs, I could feel the assumption he made about our relationship.

"It's good to see you, little lady," Mitch said, pouring Khôi a beer and a mineral water for me.

"The Commies haven't made any more trouble for you, have they?" He settled back in his armchair, beer in hand.

"Not yet," I said softly.

"You are safe, even with Khôi here," he half-joked. "You're in America. Do you like it?"

I hesitated. It felt like I'd be insulting his house to tell the truth about the loneliness I felt everywhere in what Khôi called the suburbs.

"It's not as beautiful or busy as Hanoi," Mitch said, answering his own question. "I'm so glad I chose to go with the MIA team. I did not think... I put ghosts to rest that I didn't know were bothering me still from thirty-five years ago.

It's a long time but it doesn't feel like a long time if you live it to the full."

Khôi nodded as if he knew what it was like to have fought in a war.

Mitch's wife cooked us a casserole and served the men more beer. She had stories edged in the lines of her face, and she made sure I was being looked after.

The drink loosened Mitch's tongue, and he told us the same story that I had seen in the Marble Mountains, of the Americans using audio recordings at night to spook the Viet Cong.

"I'm glad that Khôi could help you out, little lady. He's a good kid," Mitch assured me.

Khôi raised his eyebrows in annoyance, then grinned. The beer was having an effect on him too.

When we caught a cab back to his flat, Khôi was on the verge of tears. I did not know why, but when I brushed against him, I caught a flashback of him being debriefed in an office. It felt like it had happened very recently.

He had said nothing to me about his own reporting to the MIA team, I realised. Finally, I could bear the weighted silence no longer.

"Khôi, are you all right?" I asked, as we pulled into his apartment block driveway.

"Wait till we are inside," he said in Vietnamese, and he paid the driver.

Once we were in the lounge room, he collapsed on the couch.

"I'm all right. But you may not be," he blurted out. At my stunned expression, Khôi looked like he was going to cry.

"They debriefed me today. They wanted to know if I was working for the Vietnamese government. The bastards. I told them that you were my girlfriend in Việt Nam so they wouldn't ask if you were psychic or not. Then they revealed that they knew I slept on the couch. I tried to explain we were doing things the old-fashioned way. They didn't believe me. And bloody Mitch had already told them that you were a psychic." Khôi swallowed and could barely look me in the eye. "Mitch doesn't know about me. But he knows about you. He wants you to go back to Việt Nam and help more vets. They didn't ask me what you wanted. They only told me what to do about you. I'm supposed to keep an eye on you and when the time comes, they will recruit you."

"I thought Americans didn't use psychics."

"They will do what would please the vets. And Mitch is well connected."

I sat on an armchair and tried not to give in to my fear of serving more military men.

"I'll try my best to protect you, Kim. I know you didn't come to the States with me to do more retrieval work. Nor to go back to Bác Phuc. I'll try my best."

But it may not be enough, I thought, as he opened up another beer.

I stomached my disappointment and did not let myself cry until I was alone under the covers. Was there nowhere in the world that I could contact the spirits without lies or bribes?

When I fell into sleep and the grey twilight of the other shore, Bà was there. I had prayed for her at the temple in Orange County and tonight she seemed to glow.

- *How is America?* Bà asked.
- *It is bland and boring*, I told her, truthfully. *But at least I am safe, I think.*
- *It is a country without soul, though it is rich.*

Bà had put her finger on what I found missing among the concrete pavements and nature strips.

- *How is Khôi treating you?*
- *Like a gentleman*, I said.
- *He likes you and he has a good heart*, Bà told me.

I knew her words were not chosen lightly. But I could not respond in kind. Khôi had done everything for me, asking for nothing in return. I merely did the occasional reading for him.

- He has been good to me, I replied.

- That is rare, Bà said, and mercifully left it at that
about Khôi.

- How are my family? I asked her.

*- They are upset that you have not returned home yet. But I
think that when you contact them they will understand.*

I doubted this. Even though Bà was the elder she still
viewed my family through rose-tinted glasses. I knew the
truth about my parents and how they viewed my gift only
as a way to make money.

Then Bà gave me a hug and I felt my spine tingle as it did
with the dead. But inside I felt warm for the first time since
leaving Hanoi.

The next day Khôi warned me that his mother wanted to
meet me.

"Does she know I'm psychic?" I asked.

Reluctantly, he nodded.

"She wanted to know why I was endangering our relationship with the Vietnamese government. I told her..."
I looked at him curiously. He was blushing. "I told her
I was in love with you. It's almost the only thing she wants
to believe. And she doesn't want to share our position with
anyone. She isn't pleased with me right now."

"Are you in love with me?" I was astounded that anyone,
let alone someone as worldly as Khôi, would be.

Khôi gave me a quirky smile.

"I like you. But I don't want to marry you yet, so you can relax."

I laughed. Suddenly the day seemed brighter.

There was a knock on the front door and then it opened. Khôi's mother had a key to his flat. She nodded at Khôi and then she met my eye with a steady, bird-like gaze.

"My son has told me about you," she said without ceremony. She had brought a stew, which she put on the kitchen bench.

"Can you cook?"

"A little," I stammered. The maid did most of the cooking in Hanoi. I had the distinct impression that nothing I said would help her adjust to my presence.

"I heard you speak good English. The community college English classes will help you speak American English." She sat down on the couch opposite her son.

"Are you migrating here?"

I was taken aback by her bluntness.

"I'd like to." Suddenly I wondered how much she knew and how much Khôi had told her. Khôi was becoming more and more uncomfortable, and I realised she knew everything. There was no benefit to hiding things from a community leader like her.

"Hmm. You should know that you cannot easily get a Green Card to work here, even if you marry my son."

"I don't intend to…" I trailed off. This was a fruitless conversation, at least on my part.

"Your actions have cost us a good contact in the Party. Being a woman, I understand why you defected when Phuc Le tried to marry you. But defecting has a price. I can help you gain contacts so you can make a living here. But you will have to give me half your fee."

I opened my mouth and shut it again. What she was proposing would cost me more than I would gain. Khôi looked like he had been slapped.

"Ma, she needs money to live here. How do you expect her to afford it if you take such a high percentage?"

His mother held out her hand to me and I understood what I had to do.

"You don't want Khôi to spend time with me. You want him to be free to date whom he likes." I released her hand. I did not have to be psychic to know that.

"Very good. One hundred dollars. That should be enough for all three of us."

I tried to glance at Khôi, but he was looking away, embarrassed.

That night I reached out for Bà. At least there was someone from my family that would be accessible and sympathetic towards me.

- *Bà,* I called out over the other shore.

After a while Bà materialised, along with Thinh, who was still in her best clothing and holding on to a bunch of red and white carnations.

- *Little one. How are you faring in America?* Bà asked me.

Hesitantly, I told them both of how I was being used by Khôi's mother.

- *Việt Kiều have different values than Vietnamese,* Bà told me. *But this boy, he has looked after you, hasn't he?*
- *Yes, he has. He's done more for me...* "Than my parents" is what I wanted to say, but, mercifully, I kept my mouth shut.
- *Have you heard from our family?* Bà asked.
- *No. I thought they may not be able to contact me without arousing suspicion.*
- *Hmm,* Bà said, and stopped asking about them.
- *You have made some of the spirits that haunt Việt Nam able to go home and find a resting place,* Thinh said. *You have done well with your gift. Maybe you can make American spirits happy too.*

I smiled at the praise. Then I drifted off to sleep, content.

I was left on my own in the flat while Khôi was at college. Occasionally I received visitors, averaging two a week. The excursions to the other shore kept me grounded. Khôi only drank some of the time when he was at home. He taught me little tricks to stay grounded in the moment, and passed his own clients on for me to do readings. It struck me that Khôi actually didn't like being psychic and he did not need money, so he was happy to share. Unlike his mother, or my father. Maybe it was a generational thing. They had grown up lacking the financial security that we took for granted.

I could not work out whether Khôi had been telling the truth when he had said he liked me. He was certainly kind and considerate, and treated me better than any potential suitors at home. I was confused. I did not know how I felt about Khôi. His goodwill made everything possible for me. I was grateful, and whenever we met on the other shore I still got that tingle and that electric sensation when I touched his hand. But I was scared of what could happen, even though I told myself Khôi was not Bác Phuc. He was my own age, for starters, and had never threatened me.

Slowly I learnt to trust Khôi. I began to sleep better at night, knowing he was on the couch, though there seemed to be nothing to guard against in America. He gave me little tokens of kindness, taking me to places that served bành xeo, the Southern Vietnamese pancake, when had I admitted I liked it and taking me shopping for clothes with his sister. He helped out Tam too. Maybe he was looking for extra merit in his deeds. Or maybe, I admitted to myself, he liked me.

The next time I saw his mother, she rinsed out the casserole dish in which she had made sticky rice for Khôi. She didn't appear to notice that I had come out from the bedroom, but I knew she could be deceptive. I walked up and greeted her politely. I told her about the monastery destruction in Bàt Nha and she nodded. She had talked to Tam and was thinking of bringing it up with the local senator. Her business contacts were Vietnamese as well as non-Vietnamese and, as the president of the Vietnamese Business Association, her word carried weight.

But when she told me that it was all over the local Vietnamese news media I despaired. The story needed to reach the non-Vietnamese world. She sat me down with a cup of tea.

"Non-Vietnamese don't care. And second-generation Vietnamese youth don't care either," she said bluntly.

"How can you not care?" I asked, losing my temper. "The Vietnamese government is corrupt."

"Do you think America is any better?" She asked me. "You are young like Khôi. Democracy depends on compromises, dictatorships on corruption. And for the moment Việt Nam is just another cheap holiday destination for foreigners. They choose not to see." I shook my head, already regretting having lost my temper in front of her. "I didn't bring Khôi up to be an activist. I brought him up to be moderate and modest. He cares about Prajna monastery because you do."

I stared at her, aghast. I did not think I could have this effect on people. What she told me about Khôi contrasted with the young man I knew. Judging from the effort he took to hide his drinking from her, I figured that who I saw was the true Khôi, rather than the son of a community leader.

"Khôi needs to be able to return with the MIA teams. Maybe with them he can monitor what is going on internationally. You know you are probably not going to be able to go back, don't you? And your family may suffer as a result."

I wet my lips with my tongue. I had wired money back to my family, heedless of who was receiving it at the other end. I trusted that Khôi could visit them and see how they were going. Now it felt hopelessly naive.

His mother patted me awkwardly on the knee, as if to comfort me.

"Take care of my son. He means well, and he likes you a lot. I hope that you like him too, and not just because he is an American."

I nodded, stunned at her assumptions. She got up from the couch and dried off the casserole dish.

When Khôi came home later that day I found it hard to act as if nothing had happened. It was a relief when he asked me what it had been like with his mother.

"She's… concerned about you," I said, not knowing whether to tell him or not.

He sat down next to me on the couch and looked me directly in the eye, and I sensed that he had rehearsed this in his mind.

"I won't let her dictate to us what she wants. So that leaves us with the question of what we want. I'd like to get to know you better… slowly."

"I don't know," I said truthfully. I held out my hand and he took it, cool and calm.

Bending my head, I allowed Khôi to see my confusion.

"You don't have to answer now. There's a lot to take in," Khôi said, as if from a great distance.

"Okay," I said vaguely, and fell asleep, trusting, on the couch by his side.

I woke up alone to a knock on the door. I opened it to see two men in shirts and ties carrying a document giving them the right to enter Khôi's flat. They seized my upper arms and marched me out of the house without giving me a chance to call Khôi or pack any clothes. Terrified, I submitted to them, fearing that the long reach of the Vietnamese government had caught up with me.

Then I was driven to a series of buildings behind barbed wire. A large sign proclaimed the facility to be a minimum-security facility of the United States of America.

Khôi told me later that there was a hotline for people to inform the government of visa breaches. Apparently, someone didn't like me being here. Hearing this sent a shudder down my spine. That someone could mean me so much harm.

I was processed and put into detention.

14

I am Kim Nguyen. There were generations of us, going back centuries, when Việt Nam had only six names. My middle name was chosen from a line in a poem that indicates what generation I am from.

I held onto this thought like a mantra, an anchor in the chaos of my thoughts. Sometimes I tried to meditate, breathing in and out, hoping that I would discover what is memory, past, psychic, future and, most importantly, where my present is.

At times I became aware I was in a bed that wasn't my own, the flat mattress pressing up against me. Sometimes I felt surrounded by words that I barely guessed the meaning of. Sometimes I felt panic and alarm in the back of my mind, that I was somewhere I didn't want to be. But I let this fear go, because to give in would mean I'd be lost.

Where was I?

I gasped for air, my heart beating fast like a trapped sparrow. Calming myself, I breathed in, then out again. It was important for me to know, to find a location for my body and being.

Opening my eyes, I saw a flat, white ceiling. The smell of antiseptic was heavy in the room. Was I in hospital? But my body felt intact. To reassure myself, I raised my shaking hands to my eyes. My burgundy nail polish was chipped and flaking. The sight of it made me panic again. Clearly, I hadn't looked after myself for a while.

I sat up slowly, feeling the movement in my muscles. I was not restrained and I was able to look around the room. Next to me was a curtained-off area and beside that a door. The bedside table next to me was plain but modern.

A PA crackled into life. I heard a voice, but the accent was so broad I barely made out the English words. Someone was being called to reception. The bedside table had a drawer and large cupboard inside of it. Pulling open the drawer, I saw my watch and an envelope.

I grabbed the envelope for clues. I opened it and out slid out a gold chain with a jade statuette of Quan Âm. Bà's necklace! Hurriedly, I put it around my neck.

I was wearing a white hospital gown. In the cupboard I found some of my clothes: a pair of jeans, a tight pink T-shirt, sneakers and a white jumper. I put them on. My pendant swung gently against the hollow of my neck, and I grasped the cold stone for reassurance. Then I looked out the window beside the bed.

Outside there was a concrete balcony and asphalt down below. A barbed-wire fence blocked off the rest of my view. I caught a glimpse of myself in the reflection of the window. My face was bare of make-up – it was a shock to see myself without red lipstick. How long had I been here?

Sitting back on the bed, I flicked my unmanicured fingers together. *It's important to seem normal*, I thought, *then no one will suspect you.*

I was afraid to go to sleep, afraid of drowning in all those memories again, not only others' memories but mine as well. Was I in a yet another dream or was this real? I had a strong feeling that I'd seen this place before.

Determined, I sat up on the bed, hungry despite everything. I pushed open the door and caught a smell of cooking grease in the corridor. I wandered towards the cooking smells. I passed more glass doors and peeked through them on my way through. There was a glimpse of beds, and shadows of other people.

At the end of the corridor were swinging doors, opaque except for two round windows. A security camera was installed over them and there was a red alarm button shielded behind glass on the wall beside them.

I pushed one of the doors open. A clutter of benches and tables greeted my gaze, a cafeteria of sorts.

"What are you doing here? Wait for the bell," a gruff male voice snapped for my attention. Meekly, I left the food hall and turned back down the corridor.

"You're new," the gruff voice followed me and the hair on the back of my neck prickled. I turned around. A large man hovered too near to me, dark-skinned and unshaven. "Who are you?"

"Kim."

"I'm Alex. Where are you from?"

"Việt Nam." This, at least, I was sure of.

"What you in for?"

I blinked at him, knowing my answer would not make sense and that he was the sort of person used to making demands for pleasure.

"I don't know," I said defensively, then, so as not to seem rude: "I don't speak English very well."

He grunted and stared at me for a moment longer than necessary. Then he stumbled back into the food hall, the doors swinging shut behind him. His mind was shuttered from mine and the threat of violence was coiled behind his steps. I fled back to my room.

I knew that, if I let it, fear would start creeping up my spine. Once I would have welcomed the silence here, but now that I had it, I chafed with the desire to know what was going on. It seemed so long since I had the security of innocence. I longed for it, like a hungry person longs for food. I remembered where I'd seen these walls before. When the abbess held my hands. She had seen this in a future that was now my present.

My mind and thoughts were insubstantial, slippery like mist. I clutched my fingers around the jade figurine of Quan Âm for reassurance.

Form is emptiness, emptiness is form...

The door opened. I focused my gaze on a woman in a suit as she came in with her identification tag clipped to her bosom. She was accompanied by a handsome Vietnamese man in shirt and trousers. Automatically my guard went up. Reading the woman's identification card, I recognised her as a government official.

"Chào chi," the man said with a Southern accent, and the official nodded to me.

"We'll go to the interview room," she said, and the man duly translated her words.

Playing dumb, I followed them out into the corridor. My natural caution warned me not to let on I could understand everything she said. We went in the opposite direction to the café and past a common room where people in casual clothes watched TV. To my surprise there were males and females together in the same room, and a child fidgeted at the feet of one of the women.

There was tension here – the illusion of freedom.

I was shown into a small room with a glass door. A table and three orange plastic chairs furnished the room. An ever-present security camera blinked in the corner and a guard in black, truncheon hanging by his side, walked by.

We sat down. The Vietnamese man smiled at me, and I was momentarily taken aback at his openness. He seemed to fear nothing, and this made me wonder. Around his wrist was a plastic tag but he ignored it.

"My name is Nam. I'm a volunteer visitor and a registered interpreter. I'm here to ensure you have rights in this process and also to advise you on what to do."

Rights? My skin prickled. *Process? Of what?*

A *visitor*, he had said. Ah. So he was free to leave. This meant he had power.

The woman had a folder with her that she plonked on the table. She said to Nam, "Make sure she knows where she is. We've had problems trying to interview her before. The doctor isn't coming for another week. She's been sedated so she may be a bit vague."

So, I'd been drugged, then. Scared, I realised what was wrong with my mind.

Nam coughed and looked me in the eye. "Sister, do you know where you are?" he said in Vietnamese.

I looked from him to my interrogator and back. Nam was well dressed with gelled black hair. He also wore a wedding band. He was clearly a Southerner. My Northern accent would give me away. I wondered if it would be better for me to speak English.

I said, answering the question: "America."

"Do you know where in America?" This was what frightened me. I felt like I was drowning. Sedated. They had given me medication, dulling my senses. I shook my head. Saying nothing was the safest option.

"Do you know what this place is?" This was the question I wanted an answer to. If they wanted to, they would withhold the answer from me and frighten me.

"You are in a detention centre for asylum seekers," he answered his own question.

"She doesn't know where she is," he told the woman.

"Ask her where she's from, how long she's been here and how she got here." The woman's mouth thinned into an unsympathetic line. He asked the question.

"Hanoi. And I don't know."

"How can she not know?" she rapped out impatiently. "Ask her what time of day it is?"

"Daytime."

"Tell her that if she is unable to answer the questions, we will assume that she is seeking asylum illegally and we can deport her back to Việt Nam," the official said, running out of patience. Nam coughed and looked me in the eye again, willing me not to look at the official.

"If they do not know anything about you, they will send you back to Hanoi. Do you want to go back to Hanoi?"

"Khong." *No.* I was horrified by the thought.

"Do you have family here?" he asked.

"No."

"Has she been seen by a psychiatrist?" Nam asked.

"Yes, she has. He says she's delusional. I'm going to get him to assess whether she's fit to travel next week."

Nam fixed me with his gaze again and flicked back his fringe with a hand. He seemed sympathetic.

"They want to deport you back to Việt Nam. Do you want to stay in America?"

I looked at him and then at the official.

"Yes." It seemed to be the right answer, for Nam was satisfied.

"We can appeal against you being deported, but you have to talk to me about why you want to stay. Do you still see things that aren't there?"

I looked at him suspiciously. What did he mean?

"Are you well?"

"Yes. Except for my memory," I admitted to this strange Southerner, who appeared friendly.

"You need to tell them how you came here and why you want to stay. Do you remember which school you went to?"

I hesitated. "Hanoi Girls' School."

"Why do you want to stay here?"

My stomach cramped. *Because I'm afraid to go back.* Unwittingly, I had spoken my thoughts loud.

"She's afraid to return because of the government," he told the official.

My reaction must have shown on my face, for Nam had not even translated the question. He waited for me to say something more, but I'd tripped up. *Best to say nothing,* I reminded myself. *They will make up their own stories about you to cover up the silence.*

"What did you do against the government?" Nam asked. "You are safe to tell the truth and it's better if you do. America is not Communist."

"I'm a psychic," I declared and saw fear flit across Nam's face.

"What did she say?" the official demanded.

"She's a psychic," Nam translated. The official's face closed shut like a book.

"That's what she was gabbling on about before. She has delusions of grandeur. It's in our report."

"Can I see the report?" Nam asked.

"Why?" The official was suspicious.

"I am here to act as her advocate. Therefore I am entitled to see the centre's documentation on her."

"Well, then, once she's declared fit to travel, we'll deport her within twenty-eight days. That's the process. Unless she gives the tribunal something it can actually believe."

He turned back to me.

"They are going to assess you for being fit to travel. If you are fit, they will send you back to Việt Nam. You have to tell me the truth. If you are afraid, I will come back as a visitor without the representative from Immigration."

"Vang," *Yes*, I nodded in agreement.

"Right. That's all I need to say to her. The interview is over," the official said.

Nam nodded curtly and they both stood up. I sat there, stunned, until Nam gestured to me. I got to my feet slowly, like an old woman, and followed them out.

"I will see you soon," Nam said as they escorted me to my room.

I tried not to hope, watching them exit, closing the door behind them.

Mealtime passed in grey monotony. Bland food, served in silence, conversation minimal. People listless and not relaxed. The stern-eyed nurse standing near the door, monitoring us.

Afterwards, the other detainees retreated to the TV common room. I retreated to my room, trying not to panic at the gaps in my mind. I'd been distracted so far by my new surroundings. I remembered a flash of bright-blue sky. People laughing, empty spaces, wide roads and concrete footpaths. Quiet and calm like I'd never experienced in Việt Nam.

Did I want to be in America? Certainly. Thinking of Hanoi made me shrink inside.

I remembered a place called Little Saigon, a bustling, crowded marketplace with mostly Vietnamese spoken and Southern food served in the restaurants. The occasional person turning their nose up at my Northern accent.

I ventured into the common room to talk to the other detainees. The man I sat next to, skinny and sloppy in an Adidas tracksuit, turned around. He smelled of cigarette smoke.

"Feeling better now?" He spoke slowly.

"Yes," I nodded.

"I'm Mac. At least you have an advocate. No one is going to advocate for me." How did he know? Then I remembered that everyone in the common room would have seen Nam, the official, and me walk past.

"I'm waiting on appeal. Last stop before they send me back to Greece. I left there when I was two. Don't even speak the language." There was none of the guardedness in his manner I'd been used to in Việt Nam, and the others in the common room were all listening. Apathy and quiet desperation clung to the grey walls. I didn't need to hold his hand to know he was a talker.

"They are going to assess me to see if I'm fit to travel." I repeated the words that I'd been told slowly, as if English was difficult for me.

"Ah. You might be on the plane before me. You speak good English. You been here long?"

I shook my head.

"This is Amy." He introduced me to the Chinese woman who sat next to him.

In Việt Nam you never knew who could be trusted, who would talk to the authorities. Here it was, as Mac said, the last stop. Nothing left to lose. No one cared what might be said or overheard. My stomach cramped again.

"Can you really tell fortunes?" asked Amy. She was wearing a pink T-shirt and grey moccasins with loose-fitting jeans. "I want to know my fortune. I want to stay here." The desperation in her eyes warned me off the truth.

"No," I said. I'd learnt the hard way that the gift I had was loaded with responsibility, and the cornered look in Amy's daughter's eyes, her gaze flicking to mine, made my heart sink.

They were trapped. And so was I.

I went into my room, wanting to hide from the expectations of others. Then the nurse barged in.

"Pill time. You have to line up at the pharmacy." She left the room.

Pill time? I felt well. I didn't need drugs.

My mind was gradually becoming clearer. My fingers tingled. I had deliberately not held the hand of anyone at the detention centre. I wondered whether I was still prescient. If I was, I'd be able to pick up on the extra undercurrents and know what to do. What if I'd lost my gift? Panic began to flood me, and then the door opened again. The nurse stood there holding a paper cup with two white pills in it.

"You didn't get your medication. I've brought it for you this time, but you have to get it yourself next time. Pill time at eight every day."

"I'm not sick," I said in English.

"Take your medication," the nurse said. I refused to move from my chair.

"Or would you like another injection? We can get a court order and give you one, you know." She was getting impatient now and I could sense her vice-like determination even without touching her skin. Reluctantly, I left my seat and took the pills from her.

"Swallow them."

I put them in my mouth. She watched my throat as I swallowed. I knew how to throw it up later, I reassured myself.

"Good girl." She crumpled the empty paper cup in her hand. Then she walked away, leaving me standing there.

I looked up at the security camera. Cameras were in the bathroom too. I knew I wasn't sick. Maybe the pills were smothering my memory and my prescience. I lay down on the bed. I needed to test this out. I needed to touch someone. Suddenly, I wanted someone to tell me that I was real. That this was real.

Then the fuzziness set in, and my feelings drifted away slowly like melting ice. Soon I was asleep.

The next day, to my surprise, there was a PA announcement for me.

"Kim Nguyen, you have a visitor in the visitors' area."

Mac showed me how to get there, saying, "You have to go through the stress room first."

The stress room?

The grim-looking nurse was standing at the door leading to the visitors' area. I went over to her.

"I have a visitor," I said.

"We know," she said, opening the door into a small, brightly lit white room for me. Another nurse was standing there.

"Take your clothes off," the first nurse said.

"What?" I asked.

"Take your clothes off." She mimicked taking her clothes off with her hands. The other nurse started to advance on me, and I stepped back.

Frightened, I took off my cardigan. It was obvious that if I didn't do this, they would do it for me. I stripped down to my underwear and watched as the other nurse rifled through my clothes. The first nurse put her hand on my skin, and I winced at the cold.

She patted me down and I got glimpses of other bodies being patted down, and a sense of oppression, of the everyday routine. But they were only glimpses, nothing like the full revelations that I would have had before being medicated.

When I had put my clothes back on I was shaking, humiliated, for myself and those who had gone before me.

"You can go into the visitors' area now."

The nurse opened the door and I stepped out into another common room. This time there was a glass window leading to a bare courtyard. For the first time I saw a sliver of blue sky. Nam had come with a bag of oranges and I met his gaze directly.

"Why are you afraid of me?"

He started out of his pose and drew himself up. "I've read your file," he said, gesturing at the folder.

I cocked my head to one side and looked blankly at him. I wanted to ask him more, but caution warned me against admitting total ignorance. He bobbed his head to me, recognising the jade Quan Âm hanging around my neck.

He looked at the guards chatting among themselves. They wore black uniforms and truncheons hung by their sides. There was a low-grade tension among them.

He settled in his chair.

I started shivering. Ghosts were here in the detention centre. The miasma of fear and suppressed violence seeped from the walls. This was a prison.

"They'll either deport you to Việt Nam or you will be granted a visa to stay here."

I blinked at him.

"How did you arrive here? The papers say you have overstayed your tourist visa, which expired six months ago. You must have some connections here." I shrugged. His voice dropped to a lower tone. "We need reliable psychics here. Tell me what you think of me."

Resentment rose in me. He did not really care about me at all, only my gift. And, like all men, he would be prepared to do anything to own it.

But I wanted out of the detention centre, and so I held out my hand and he took it firmly, smiling into my eyes. Like most men, he thought a lot of himself. But he was a good man. He worked as a volunteer translator. He had seen clothes-makers go through the detention centre and had not been able to do much for them because they had no money… He had been born in Việt Nam and, like many Southern Vietnamese, had escaped on a boat. He was lucky that the American government at the time had welcomed Vietnamese refugees. Not like now. He felt guilty that I was in detention while he had avoided a similar fate.

"You were unable to help the others that were here before me," I said, looking into his face. He dropped my hand and looked away.

"I will do my best for you," he said, "but you have to tell me everything."

I peered at him over my caution. *He is genuine*. I took a breath and began.

"So why did you come here?" Nam asked me as I finished talking and took a sip of orange soft drink.

"They were still watching me," I explained. My head began to clear as I spoke in Vietnamese. The shadows in the visitors' room were beginning to lengthen and I knew he would have to go soon. I did not have to explain anymore.

"You still have your gift?"

"Yes," I said crossly, "but it's fuzzy now. From the pills, I think. If only I could stop taking the pills."

"But they are still going to deport you unless you can come up with a plausible story for them. The immigration authorities don't believe in psychics, and they don't believe the Bureau exists."

Frustrated, I looked out into the bare enclosed courtyard. "I thought in a democracy you could tell the truth." As the words came out of my mouth, I realised how naive I sounded. "I didn't think I would end up in prison in America…"

Nam looked away, thinking. "You could lie. You could say that your family has Southern connections, and you couldn't get work, then you might be considered an economic refugee. Or you could marry an American citizen." Revulsion pulsed across my face and Nam gave a wry smile. "Maybe not. Your psychiatric assessment is tomorrow. Lie to them, so they stop giving you the pills. Pretend you are not gifted anymore – to them you appear psychotic. Think of a story tonight. Speak only Vietnamese to the officials. Some broken English would be all right, though."

"You know Mac?"

"I know most of the current detainees," Nam said quietly.

"You don't think… that the Communists have a reach out here?"

Nam looked at me strangely. "I wouldn't like to think so," he said. "The feeling against the Vietnamese government is very strong among the older generations here."

That evening I lined up obediently for my pills. When I was handed them, I swallowed, then went to the bathroom, stuck my fingers down my throat and threw them up.

My head was clearer and I felt better for it.

The next morning I returned to myself, slowly, as if waking up from a nightmare. I breathed in and out, trying to calm my racing heart. I felt sick to the stomach. My own memories unfolded and became too much. My stomach lurched and I ran to the bathroom. I retched until I threw up nothing but bile and water.

Someone knocked on the door. Petrified, I stayed in the bathroom. But then they came in anyway, and called out in Vietnamese.

"Em?" An old woman's voice. She was dressed in a baggy brown jumper and glasses – just another old woman.

"Bà…" I said, not knowing what to do. She reached out to clasp my hands and I withdrew from her touch.

"Will they send me back?" I asked her. The old woman's face folded in on herself and tears leaked from her eyes. "If you are here, they will send you back." She started to shake and, belatedly, I remembered my manners. I escorted her to sit on my bed.

"Why are you…"

The old woman looked at me. "My nephew… he uses heroin. I let them put me in jail instead. He is young and has much more life. I thought I would only go to jail. But they stripped me of my residency and now…" Her fear was infectious. She would be punished, like me. "There is an interpreter who comes and visits. He says I can appeal. At least in jail here I can see my nephew. He visited me. But he will not go to Việt Nam. I am old. My suffering is near the end."

She straightened up, as if suddenly remembering I was a stranger, and fearing she had said too much.

"What did you do?"

"I want to stay here," I said in a meek voice. I couldn't burden this old woman with any more troubles.

"Are you feeling better now? The food here is terrible," the old woman said. Her kindness almost brought me to tears again. This was a Southerner, our enemies, who betrayed their own people. But all I could see then was how much this woman cared for those she loved, and the strangers around her like me.

"Have a rest," she assured me, patting the bed. She made me lie down and only then did she shuffle out of the room and shut the door.

I closed my eyes. My head seemed clearer now that I was grounded in the present. Just like being in Hanoi, except that here was the possibility of release from conditions, Nam had explained. Governments change in America and there was always the possibility of change in a democracy, Nam had assured me when I had raised my eyebrows in disbelief.

"There are things wrong in America. But at least we may be able to get you free with an appeal without bribing anyone," he had added philosophically.

The bureaucracy here had no face. I would never be able to touch the hands of those that would decide my fate. I could not foresee my future, but at least my head was clear.

That night, undrugged, I felt my gift unfurl in the darkness of my room. The centre reeked of despair, and I found it hard to keep myself afloat in the morass of human feeling.

Somehow, even though I had tried to flee Việt Nam, I was still imprisoned. Tears choked up in my throat and I muffled myself with a hand.

I clutched at the jade Quan Âm around my neck, returning to the island of peace within.

I tried to touch my emotions, my fears threatening to cascade into tears like broken glass.

Then I found myself on the other shore. Khôi was waiting for me.

- *I'll be there soon,* Khôi promised, and nodded to me.

With that I drifted fully off to sleep, lulled into the safety of the other shore.

The days seemed to spiral into long stretches of nothingness. I could not stay asleep and hope to reside for long periods on the other shore. I was too overwhelmed by the tragic stories of the other refugees. We were all caught in a legal system we barely understood.

Where were Khôi and Tam? Did they know where I was? Surely Khôi, if not his mother, would have contacts. Nam did know Khôi's mother, and I had asked him to inform her son of where I was. Nam seemed honourable enough – surely my message would have been passed on?

The nights were hard. If I took the tablets given to me, I would sleep, but I would not see the other shore. Anxiety kept me awake and my mind telescoped into fear of being sent back into Bác Phuc's custody.

The rules of America viewed me as a child, and American beliefs about psychics kept me out of Bác Phuc's clutches for the moment. I did not feel like a child anymore. Feeling the experiences of others had lost me my innocence.

When Khôi finally came, I took one look at him and burst into tears. When he hugged me, I realised how much I missed friendly human touch, even though I had only been in detention a week at most.

"Kim, I'm sorry it took me so long. My mother was involved in some discussions about you. I had to get Mitch to tell her what you did in the Marble Mountains for her to see what a contribution you could make to our community here. What she suggested was…" Khôi looked away from me for a second and I realised what they were going to propose. "She asked me if I'd mind marrying you. It can be a secular ceremony here with a celebrant of no faith. I would view it as a paper formality, nothing more. We can still sleep separately…"

He was babbling and I gently touched his hand. I saw how mortified he was, his secret hope that I could love him, and how embarrassed he was by this supposed fake marriage.

"It's okay, Khôi. I know." I looked into his face and saw he was blushing again. He knew it was too soon to expect me to fall in love with him or to love him. Encouraged by what I saw in his mind, I touched his cheek with a finger. "I don't mind marrying you," I said. I did not speak aloud what was in my mind – that I would suicide rather than be subject to Bác Phuc again.

Khôi laughed.

"This is the most unromantic place to have a wedding. I never imagined that it would be this way."

"Nor I," I said and felt the tears build up in my eyes. I imagined that when I got married it would be beautiful, with a white dress and my family and friends around me. Instead it would be walled in by grey and an atmosphere of despair.

"I didn't intend to be married at seventeen either. My mother said I can annul it later if I need to."

Suddenly I saw through his eyes the respect and resentment he had for his mother, successful and resourceful. This American boy had had no idea about the wars until he had worked as an MIA liaison. Just like me.

Marriage to him was a foreign country. At least we knew how to live around each other, even if not in a romantic sense.

"You could annul it too…" he added hastily, and I could not suppress a smile.

The warmth I had been feeling towards Khôi seemed to intensify.

"Khôi. Thank you for your generous offer. Of course I accept. Any girl would be lucky to be with you…" I fumbled around with the formality of the words. How could I make him not feel obliged towards me, in a marriage he did not seek out?

"I like you. I like you a lot. And maybe we will learn more about each other in the few years we have to stay together till you get American citizenship. Then you will be free to go." Khôi's words sounded rehearsed. But at the end he met my eye and smiled, and my doubts evaporated.

For the first time we held hands and in a kaleidoscopic moment I saw how he perceived me, a young girl haloed in bright light who could read his mind and not criticise him for it. He saw my perception of him, and I felt him blush further.

Both of us being psychics meant we had to be even more respectful of each other. He let go of my hand then, as if we had come too close.

"It will be different being with you. I don't know what my friends will think. And we did not know whether I should have asked your family. Would you like me to?"

"They don't know where I am. Have you heard from them?"

I had managed to stretch a short trip into several months without them questioning me.

"I haven't. I did not want to jeopardise them, with a Communist Party member having tabs on them."

A chill ran down my spine. I did not feel I had managed to get away from Bác Phuc yet, although a solution had presented itself.

"All my friends think that I met a child bride from Việt Nam," he continued. "You will meet them all once you are out. Mother would like a proper, large reception with her friends, family, cousins and the like. She will also have it known that you are psychic. The MIA crowd will be there too."

"Do you think that becoming American will protect me? And my family can come over?"

Khôi hesitated and I wished I hadn't asked. I wanted a happy ending. But it was unlikely to happen.

"We won't know unless we try," he said, instead of reassuring me.

That evening in bed I pretended I was being held in Khôi's arms. The sound of the air-conditioning was the buzz of mopeds around Hoan Kiem Lake. I could still taste on my tongue the sticky rice that Khôi had brought from his mother's kitchen to me. Somehow this place would have to become home to me. Then I thought of my family and tears moistened my cheeks. I wanted to get married with my family giving me away. I wanted Ngoc and Dao in the bridal party, and I wanted to attend Ngoc's wedding.

But what I wanted and what I needed were different things. I had to get out of detention and away from Bác Phuc.

Khôi organised the wedding. In attendance was Khôi's mother, Nam, Mitch and the other detainees. Khôi's mother came up with a simple white debutante dress for me after Khôi gave her my dress size. What I felt were the absences, of the people and the cheer, that had accompanied my sister's wedding. There was no champagne, just fizzy grape juice. The other refugees seemed happy for me, though they didn't know me. They could relate to my circumstances. And to my surprise Khôi's mother presented me with a silver necklace with rubies, a Vietnamese wedding custom.

Mitch provided us with two gold rings. I gladly accepted another hug from him. Khôi's mother was more circumspect, with a peck on the cheek. Even from the imprint of her lips I received a flash of her fondness of her son. There was no disappointment that she was witness to a sham marriage. Instead she was glad that Khôi had a chance to settle down.

Rebelliously and stupidly, I resented that simple thought. We were too young to be married and ought to be out on the town, enjoying ourselves like regular teenagers. Instead I sipped too-sweet grape juice, listening to his mother's opening speech.

I had to get out of this facility, I told myself when my thoughts wandered elsewhere. Living with Khôi was not my worst fate. He was a good boy.

When the ring exchange took place, tears filled my eyes. The flashes of Khôi I felt were filled with trepidation and uncertainty. But he liked me, I could tell, even without knowing his inner mind. Like when his stare captured me like a camera and his smile seemed to emerge from within him.

But today I missed my family and friends. I felt smothered like with a blanket, though I knew it was for my benefit. The gold ring was tight around my finger. When Khôi was told to kiss the bride, I raised my lips to his. I told myself it was not just in gratitude.

Like all gifts, it came with a price.

Acknowledgements

To Liz Kemp, Anna Mandoki and Margaret Bearman, for their feedback and encouragement. Gail Jones, Nicholas Jose, Maria Tumarkin and Jamie Coleman, for valuable advice. Also many thanks to the Australian Council for the Arts, Asialink, Footscray Community Arts Centre, Glenfern, Writers Victoria, Toby Eady, the Goethe Institute, Copyright Agency Limited, Varuna Writers Centre and the University of Western Sydney, for rooms and inspiration. Thank you to Gold SF and Larissa Lai for their votes of confidence in my work. And, last but not least, thank you to my family and my partner, Alister Air, for being there.

The Other Shore was first published in Australia by Seizure Press in 2014. Thank you to David Henly for his ongoing support and work.

This edition is dedicated to the memory of Thich Nhat Hanh "Thay," who passed away in 2022. Long live his continuation – from Awakening Embrace of the Heart (dharma name of Hoa Pham).